READING THE BONES

Sheila Finch

D0117352

READING
THE BONES

Sheila Finch

Tachyon Publications
San Francisco, California

This is a work of fiction. All events portrayed in this book are fictitious, and any resemblance to real people or events is purely coincidental.

READING THE BONES

copyright © 2003 by Sheila Finch

Cover illustration by Michael Dashow

Type design by Montage

All rights reserved, including the right to reproduce this book, or portions thereof, in any form.

Tachyon Publications
1459 18th Street #139
San Francisco, CA 94107
(415) 285-5615

Edited by Jacob Weisman

ISBN: 1-892391-08-2

First Edition: September 2003

Printed in the United States of America by Phoenix Color, Corporation

0   9   8   7   6   5   4   3   2   1

For David Yates,
brother-in-heart

Acknowledgements

The author would like to thank the following people who contributed so much to this work: Patrick Price, who first encouraged me to tell the tales of the Guild of Xenolinguists; Gregory Benford who has long supported my work; Jacob Weisman, who gave good advice on this particular tale; Jerry Hannah and the members of the Asilomar Writers Consortium, without whose loving support and fierce attention to craft for more than twenty years, very little of what I write would be fit to print. My pantheon of personal gods is not responsible for the failings of this book.

PART ONE

THE OTHER SIDE OF LIGHT

ONE

Someone was trying to tell him something.

Ries Danyo wallowed round on the bench, peering through the tavern's thick haze, eyes unfocused by too much *zyth*. The sitar he didn't remember setting on the bench beside him crashed to the floor. The gourd cracked as it hit stone.

A male Freh sat beside him, the alien's almost lipless mouth moving urgently. The Freh had a peculiar swirling design tattooed from his forehead down the nose, and one of his hands was wrapped in a filthy rag. Ries stared at dark blood seeping through the folds. The alien spoke again, the pitch of his voice writhing like smoke.

Ries didn't catch a word.

Sometimes he wondered if the native vocalizations on this planet should even be called anything as advanced as language — especially the impoverished version the Freh males used. Not that his human employers were interested in actually having a conversation with these aliens. Just as well. He wasn't the lingster he'd been just five years ago.

The native liquor had given him a pounding headache and he needed to sleep it off.

The Freh's unbandaged, bird-claw hand shook his arm, urging him to pay attention. Dizziness took him. For a moment, he drifted untethered in a matrix of protolanguage, unable to grasp either the alien's Frehti or his own native Inglis to form a reply, a sensation closely resembling what he remembered of the condition lingsters called interface but without the resolution.

A harsh burst of noise battered his eardrums, booming and

echoing around the low-roofed tavern. He squinted, trying to clear his clouded vision. Two male Freh capered across the floor, arms windmilling. He started to rise —

And was knocked down off his chair and dragged behind the overturned table.

Thuds. Screams. The crowded tavern erupted into shrill pandemonium. Freh voices ululating at the upper end of the scale. Something else — a deeper footnote that brought the hairs up on his neck.

He tried to stand. The room cartwheeled dizzily around him. A pungent odor filled his nostrils — a stench like rotten flesh, decaying fungus. He had a sudden image of nightmare beasts rutting. The meal he'd just eaten rushed back up into his throat.

Something slammed into his back, toppling him again. He struggled out from underneath the weight. A pudgy juvenile Freh, shapeless in layers of thick, stinking rags, stared down at him for a moment, then scrambled away hastily. Ries sat on the floor in the wreckage, his head throbbing, his mind blank.

Tongues of flame flickered across the low ceiling; acrid smoke filled his lungs and made him cough. The coughing caused him to retch again. He doubled over.

"Talker." The alien with a bloody hand shook his arm. "Talker. Danger."

The sound of Frehti was like birdsong. Trying to make sense of such warbling, twittering, and chirruping — problematic at the best of times — was impossible in his present state. He got maybe one Frehti word in every two.

He closed his eyes against the stinging smoke, the piercing screeches. *Maybe I really am dying,* he thought.

No exaggeration. Maybe not tonight, or tomorrow, or even a month from now. But he sensed his body succumbing to death little by little, felt the slow tightening of *zyth*'s grip around his heart. He had a sudden vision — a splinter view of green foothills and sapphire lake — that closed down as rapidly as it opened. If he didn't give it up, he wouldn't live long enough to see Earth again.

Then he was aware of the bump and scrape of being hauled over benches, broken crockery, other bodies in the way.

He was too tired to resist.

TWO

One of the aliens had tried to give him a message last night.

The memory pricked him as he dropped a step behind the Deputy Commissioner's wife and her companions moving through the cloth merchants' bazaar. He shielded the flask of *zyth* he was opening from their sight and took a medicinal gulp. The demon that lived in that flask raced through his blood like liquid flame, and he felt his heartbeat quicken.

In his experience, stone sober or drunk like last night, the Freh had the most stunted language of any sentient beings in the Orion Arm. Even very early linguists from pre-Guild days had taught there was no such thing as a primitive language, and what was true on Earth had proved true through the Orion Arm: All languages the Guild of Xenolinguists had ever found were as sophisticated as their speakers needed. On the other hand, the Guild could be wrong; Frehti, the language spoken here on Krishna, could turn out to be an exception.

His head pounded as if he'd slammed it repeatedly into a stone wall, his skin was clammy, and his throat seemed to have been scrubbed with sand. He had no recollection of how he got back to his quarters in New Bombay.

It was not yet noon, but the heat was already fierce. Dust rose as he walked, making his eyes water. He sneezed, startling a small cloud of insects hovering about his face. Already he could smell the rich, chocolate odor of the river moving sluggishly past the edge of the native town. The monsoon would be here any day, bringing its own set of problems. There were no pleasant seasons on Krishna.

The native name for the planet was Not-Here. *"How can anybody say their own world isn't here?"* the Deputy Commissioner's wife had demanded when he'd translated this for her. *"No wonder they're all so useless!"* Krishna was too benign a deity to give name to this planet, he thought. Kali would've been more appropriate.

The DepCom's wife and fifteen-year-old daughter moved slowly down the line of stalls in the silk merchants' section, followed by the wife of some minor official in the human colony. The women dabbed sweat from their cheeks with one hand, fended off flying insects with the other. They took their time, the DepCom's spoiled daughter plucking with obvious irritation at her mother's sleeve. The girl's red hair which she'd piled on her head in a style much too old for her had come loose, and he could see damp strands of it stuck to the back of her slender neck.

The bazaar was crowded with small, plump aliens whose skin had a color and texture that reminded him of scrubbed potatoes. The males' faces were decorated with tattoos, crude as a child's scribbled designs, done in dark purple ink; the females went unadorned. Like many species he'd seen in the Orion Arm, the Freh were humanoid, as if once having found a good recipe, Mother Nature was loathe to throw it away, and no taller than ten-year-old human children. Their mouths had almost no lip, and their eyes were round and lacked lids. Like a bird or a reptile, they had a nictitating membrane that could veil their gaze, and their hands were four-fingered. The oddest thing about them was that such lumpish beings had mellifluous, birdlike voices.

Almost all of them here in the bazaar were male. They squatted along the edges of the narrow path between the stalls, leaned on poles supporting tattered silk awnings, or crowded around the stalls of foodsellers. Two-thirds of the male population never seemed to have anything to do; their sole purpose in life seemed to be standing about half-naked, staring at each other and at the humans.

No more details surfaced from the events in the tavern. When he'd been younger, he'd bounced back vibrantly from nights like last night. Now they left him feeling a hundred years old, his body demanding more of what was killing it to function at all. He took another sip — the alcohol flamed in his throat — put the flask back in his pocket and caught up with the women.

He despised these shopping trips. The women argued and disparaged and forced the prices down to a level he was ashamed to translate. And then they'd take their shimmering purchases back up to the Residence and have something fussy made out of them. The DepCom's women liked the delicate textiles on Krishna, but they preferred the elaborate fashions they remembered from Earth, however inappropriate they might be in this climate. But even that wasn't the heart of his discontent. This was no job for a lingster, even one who'd fallen as far as he had.

Ragged awnings over each stall hung limp in the still air. The ever-present smells of the bazaar, rotting vegetables, flyblown meat, sewage running in open ditches behind the stalls, and the merchants' sweat-soaked rags filled his nose. A hand dimpled like a child's plucked at his sleeve, and he turned to see half-raw meat on a stick offered to him. The seller of the meat gazed at him.

He recognized a juvenile, still carrying the rolls of fat about its neck that marked immaturity. Behind the juvenile, rows of small, featherless, flying creatures the natives trapped were set to roast over a bed of coals alongside succulent red-brown tubers. He shook his head and regretted it when the hangover pounded again in his temples. The juvenile grinned. There was a youthfulness in all their faces, a bland childlike expression that never seemed to mature. The only difference between them as they grew was that while they stayed pudgy, they tended to lose the exaggerated neck fat.

He'd never seen an old Freh, male or female, or even an obviously middle-aged one. He didn't know if this meant they died young, if they simply kept their old out of sight, or even if they put them all to death above a certain age. It was a mark of how little importance humans placed on the natives of this world, their customs or their language, that no xenoanthropologists had spent time here, and the xenolinguists initially sent by the Guild had spent precious little.

Across the alluvial plain on which the Freh town was built,

Krishna's sun climbed the Maker's Bones till the eroded mountains glowed fiercely white like the skeleton of some extinct mammoth. He wiped a trickle of sweat from his neck, willing the women to hurry up. Sometimes they could go on like this for a couple of hours, examining bolts of iridescent material, picking and complaining.

The squatting merchants held their wares up silently, gazing incuriously at the human women, occasionally scratching simple marks on small squares of damp clay to keep track of their sales. They had no written language, and their arithmetic, on a base of eight, seemed not to be very flexible either. He glanced at an alien infant lying in a makeshift cradle underneath a stall; its parent paid no attention or perhaps was too lazy to swat the insects swarming over its face. The DepCom's wife had organized a wives' committee to teach Krishna's natives elementary hygiene; it didn't seem to be having much success.

"Danyo." Mem Patel crooked a finger at him. "See that bolt? Find out what this shifty-eyed thief wants for it."

For this elementary task the DepCom's wife required the expensive services of a Guild lingster. Mem Patel, like the rest of the human colony, hadn't bothered to learn anything of this language beyond "Kitchen Frehti," an impoverished pidgin of a very few alien words and her own native Inglis which she used with the female Freh who worked in the Residence.

"Danyo! The brocade this boy's holding!"

Beside the male alien, a female stood up, ready to bargain. She wore a shapeless brown garment and a necklace of plaited vines with a few grey clay beads that was no match for the garish blue designs on her mate's face. On Krishna it seemed to be the female's job to communicate; he wondered if perhaps males found it beneath their dignity to talk too much.

Before he could begin, the comlink the DepCom insisted he wear on these outings buzzed at his wrist. He held the tiny receiver to his ear.

"*Ries. I need you up here. Right away.*" Deputy Commissioner Chandra Patel's voice echoed inside his skull, disturbing the brooding hangover again as if it were a flock of bats.

Ries stared at his shaking hand. "Sir?"

"*Intelligence just in,*" the DepCom's voice said. "*Mules massing across Separation River.*"

In the little more than two years Ries had been here, he'd seen the pattern repeat every year. A handful of the second race on Krishna, nicknamed "Mules" by the humans from their long, horsey faces, came into the native town and ran wild for a few days just before the monsoon struck. Nothing serious, as far as anyone could tell. A few fights with their Freh neighbors, an occasional native shack burned to the ground. One of the DepCom's hobbies had been gathering information, anecdotal for the most part, about the Mules.

"It's monsoon weather, the silly season," Ries said, watching the women plucking fretfully at rainbow silks. "Mules don't pay attention to New Bombay."

"*Maybe. But I found a record of an attack when the colony was founded fifteen years ago. Almost wiped them out.*"

The DepCom's daughter turned and, catching Ries's gaze on her, stuck her tongue out at him. He frowned at the girl and saw her laugh.

"The early commissioners kept very poor records," Patel said. "Maybe we can't trust them. But I don't want to take chances."

"Nothing the *Star of Calcutta* can't take care of, surely?"

"*Bring the women back to the Residence, Ries. Immediately.*"

THREE

The DepCom's women hadn't been pleased. Ries had let their indignation wash over him, ignoring their shrill protests.

Back in his own quarters in the Residence, he poured a shot of *zyth* in a small glass. They'd been wrong at the Mother House to think he couldn't handle it. There was a lot of pressure in lingstering; some of the Guild's best people broke under the strain.

He leaned down to the computer on his desk and touched a key; the screen became a mirror. The action reminded him how long since he'd used the AI for the purpose it was intended; hours spent browsing through its copious files on the flora and fauna of Krishna didn't count. It was as superfluous here as he felt himself to be. A highly-trained lingster and a superior AI with nothing to do, what a waste.

He frowned at his swollen face under tangled curls of dark brown hair — no grey showing yet — the line of his cheekbones blurred under the flushed skin, the blue eyes bloodshot like the tracks of a wounded bird over snow. He stepped away and noticed an extra couple of kilos around the waist.

He changed into fresh tropical whites, tugged a comb through his hair, erased the mirror, and went out of his room. At the top of the stairs, he changed his mind, ducked back inside and grabbed the flask which he tucked into a thigh pocket.

On the ground floor, a Freh houseboy with no understanding of how a central air system worked had left the doors of the Residence's great entrance hall wide open. A faint breath of humid air moved sluggishly inside, already laced with aerosols from the distant ocean's seasonal diatom bloom. Soon the monsoon would turn the streets of human enclave and native town alike into rivers of mud and the air into a smothering blanket laden with infection. He closed the doors.

Turning back, he found one of the houseboys silently moving across the hall. This one was draped in gaudy layers of red and orange silk. But today something fierce slid through the houseboy's small eyes before it was replaced by the servile, grinning expression the Freh adopted in human presence.

An arched alcove revealed a closed door. Ries knocked.

"Come in."

Chandra Patel glanced up from a large desk dominated by an oversized screen. The only sign of luxury here was the antique scarlet-and-gold carpet with a design of thatched huts and water buffalo that lay on the polished wood floor. Purchased from an impoverished museum in India and imported at great cost, it soothed Patel's occasional bouts of homesickness.

On the desk today Ries saw an uncharacteristically disorderly heap of papers, infocubes, and disks, as if the DepCom had lost patience and banged a fist down in their midst, jumbling them. The usually immaculate diplomat hadn't taken time to shave this morning, and the burgundy silk lounging robe he wore looked as if he'd slept in it.

"What haven't you told me?" Ries asked.

Across the room, Patel's tea kettle on a hot-stone and two cups of delicate porcelain waited on a small table. Ries took a pinch of aromatic black tea leaves from a canister, put one into each cup, then filled the cups with boiling water. Back turned to the DepCom, he poured a few drops of *zyth* from the flask into his own tea. He handed the other cup to the DepCom.

Patel said heavily, "The *Calcutta*'s on training maneuvers. Out of the sector. It'll take too long for her to get back."

Tea forgotten for a moment, Ries stared at the DepCom. When humans had first arrived on this planet, the Freh who lived mainly in the lowlands along Separation River had been easily impressed by the display of superior technology into letting the humans settle peacefully.

The DepCom was fond of pointing out that most Freh were living better now than they'd been before the advent of human colonists. Not to mention the stuff they managed to steal from the humans they worked for, his wife would add; colony wives had developed the necessary ritual of inventorying household property at least once a month.

The Mules seemed to be a different species than the Freh. Almost nothing was known about their history or their culture; their only observed behavior was this once-a-year mayhem visited on their neighbors. Ries himself had never even seen one close up. But the purpose of the small starship, the *Star of Calcutta*, was mainly to guard the planet against attack by the Venatixi, an alien species who bore no love for humans and whose violence intermittently scarred this sector of the Arm. Yet it seemed somebody had blundered, having the ship gone right now.

"But that isn't why I called you down here, Ries. Look at this." The DepCom indicated the screen with a brown hand. "I know you're interested in the Freh language. I think I've found something more bizarre."

Curious, Ries moved over to the desk to look. The one thing that had made his employment here bearable was Patel's friendship. It was the DepCom who suggested Ries make use of the sitar that had been his. The sitar, Ries remembered now, that had been damaged and then forgotten in a native tavern.

Before Patel could elaborate on what he'd found, the door opened and his wife hurried in. Nayana Patel — a short woman who might've been voluptuous in her youth — had changed into an elaborate red gown with voluminous skirts heavily embroidered in silver. He could see hints of the gown's Indian ancestry, but over-ornamented and fussy; the embroidery must've added at least a kilo to its weight.

"Chan!" she said sharply to her husband. "You must say something to the servants. Amah ruined my breakfast this morning. You'd think after all this while she'd have learned how to prepare naan. Now I find that she's run away."

Nayana Patel called all the female house servants "Amah,"

refusing to learn their names in retaliation for what she saw as their refusal to prepare the vegetarian diet the Patels followed, and claiming she couldn't tell one from another in any case.

"Find yourself another servant, Naya."

Half a dozen silver bracelets on her wrist chimed musically as she moved in front of his desk. "That's what I'm trying to tell you, Chan. They've all gone."

Patel stared at her for a second, then abruptly turned back to his desk and pressed a button on a small pad. They waited in silence. He banged his hand on the pad again. Nothing happened.

"You see?" Mem Patel said. "We're alone in this great awful house. Left to fend for ourselves."

Remembering the odd, veiled look the houseboy had given him, Ries felt a tremor of apprehension slide up his spine.

"Ries." Patel said. "Get my family to the *Calcutta*'s base. Take my skipcar."

Mem Patel said petulantly, "I'm not going anywhere without you, Chandra."

"Stop arguing for once, Naya, and go with Ries. I'll follow as soon as I can."

She stared at him. "But I need to pack —"

"Get the children." Patel took her arm and steered her out the door. When she'd gone, he gazed at Ries. "I can trust you with my family, can't I?"

"Sir?"

"You're a good man when you're not drinking," Patel said bluntly.

Anger burned in his stomach. "You can rely on me."

FOUR

"The bottom line, Ries," Magister Kai had said, "is that we can't rely on you anymore."

The Head of the Mother House of the Guild of Xenolinguists had turned his gaze out the arched window of his study as if autumnal rainclouds slowly obliterating Alpine peaks absorbed his full attention. Ries had been summoned back to the Mother House for retraining, something all lingsters were encouraged to do at regular intervals. Other lingsters caught up on new technology and techniques, but he was subjected to lectures from a new Head, a man less inclined to be indulgent than the one he'd known as a student twenty years ago.

"I see from the record that the Guild has given you a number of chances over the last three years." Magister Kai turned to face him again. "You were a very talented lingster in the beginning. But your addiction to native alcohols is a serious problem."

"It's under control now, Magister." What choice did he have but stay to sober on Earth? They would've found and confiscated his supply at the port if he'd tried to bring any home with him.

"Is it, Ries? I'd like to think so. I'd like to think that all the years the Guild spent preparing you for service haven't been wasted after all. I'd like to believe that we could send you out into the field without worrying whether or not you'd be sober enough to do your job. But I find that belief hard to sustain."

His last assignment had been a disaster. He knew the Guild would've much preferred to send someone other than himself, but the client alien had expressed urgency, and he'd been the only experienced lingster close enough to take the assignment at the time.

"I was sick. Picked up some kind of native virus —"

"And dosed it with native alcohol," Magister Kai said. "Dangerously compromising the interface because you were out of control. Another time you, and the Guild, may not be so lucky. You do realize the risk you take?"

Lingstering was more of an art than a science for all the Guild proclaimed otherwise, and as an artist he'd found that some native liquors set his considerable talent free. That last time he'd managed to scare himself because it had taken him days to shake the demons that stalked through his skull.

There were hazards to mixing alcohol or any pharmaceutical, alien or otherwise, with the already volatile drugs of interface. The Guild had long ago learned to weed out candidates with sensitivity to Terran intoxicants, narcotics, stimulants, and hallucinogens, not even bothering to send them for treatment. Yet it was impossible to know in advance all the alien substances a human could become addicted to and develop appropriate immunogens.

He'd begun the slide three years earlier when his young wife died. He'd promised her he'd be the rock under her feet; instead he'd let her die. The Guild told him there would've been nothing he could've done for Yv, even if he'd been there. There was nothing anybody could've done, they said. He didn't believe them; the Guild didn't approve of lingsters marrying. He'd been out of it on some native potion that morning, incapable of helping her when she needed him. Later, he drank to forget the damage the drinking had caused. And then he'd found he couldn't stop. The Guild had moved him from planet to planet, and on each he'd found something to ease his pain, something they couldn't immunize him against in advance. He didn't need some sanctimonious representative of the Guild telling him he should quit; he knew it. But he knew he wasn't ready just yet.

He said tersely, "I'm sober now."

"Perhaps you mean it this time." Magister Kai gazed at him for a moment. "And because of that, I'm giving you one last chance. The colony on Krishna was founded a dozen years ago. The aboriginal

FOUR   23 population is placid with the rudiments of a simple language. The lingsters who forged the interface set up the AI to handle it."

"Then why does anybody still need a lingster?"

"The Deputy Commissioner on Krishna, Chandra Patel, is an old friend of mine," Magister Kai said. "He wants a personal translator for his family."

FIVE

Shopping facilitator was more like it, he thought, as he left the DepCom's study. There wasn't even enough work here for a grade one translator. But he'd kept his word to Magister Kai. He hadn't missed a day of this boring and demeaning duty.

He crossed the hall. Through the high windows he saw the first wisps of cloud gathering over the jagged ribcage of the Maker's Bones. If Patel was right and the Mules intended to attack the human compound this time while the ship was offworld, there'd be real trouble.

He entered his own room and gazed at the mess he lived in. While the DepCom's wife packed, he'd better pull together a few things of his own. The only object of real importance he possessed was the fieldpack of interface drugs that all lingsters carried when they were on assignment. Not that he'd had any opportunity to use either the alpha or beta sequences in the whole two years he'd spent on Krishna, but no lingster ever walked off and left his fieldpack behind.

He thought of apocryphal stories of lingsters who'd come through disasters, triumphantly hefting their packs as if they'd faced nothing more than a routine interface. The stories were more propaganda than actual history, but the habit lingered. He strapped it on the hip opposite the flask.

To himself at least, he had to admit that he'd loved the Guild once, when he was young. He still thought with fondness of his student days. It had seemed an almost holy endeavor to immerse himself in the mystery of language, and the Guild, monastic in its foundation in any case, did little to discourage this religious fervor in its lingsters. Yet there was something about the Guild that ate up a lingster's productive years, then spat him out, exhausted, cynical and bereft.

Somewhere in the silent house he heard a muffled thud. Mem Patel, probably, bumping a trunk full of expensive clothes and baubles, and he'd be the one stuck with carrying it up to the roof. In a sour mood, he started up the stairs that led to the family's private apartments.

Another thump, behind him this time. Then a sharp crash of furniture overturned. And a scream.

He turned back too fast, triggering a giddy spell. For a second the stairs tilted crazily under his feet and he lost his footing, slipping down two steps. He grabbed at the stair rail for balance, then moved with great care across the hall till the dizziness subsided. The noise was coming from Patel's study.

Nausea rose in his stomach. He hesitated outside the door. Another scream.

He flung the door open on a nightmare scene and came instantly, sharply sober.

The DepCom lay on the antique carpet by his desk, the spreading pool of his blood obliterating its pastoral designs. One of Patel's hands clutched the shattered keypad of his terminal. Standing over him, a small, naked alien, with a face so covered in tattoos that the natural color of the skin hardly showed, held a blade like an elongated thin pyramid in one bloodstained hand.

It took Ries several seconds to comprehend the incredible scene. Not Mule. The assassin was Freh. His heart lurched.

The plump little alien glanced at Ries. Two others, wearing only the Freh version of a loincloth, were ransacking the room, overturning chairs and emptying bookshelves.

He screamed at them in Kitchen Frehti: "Scum, obey your master." Lingster or not, it was all he could remember of the language in his shock.

The Freh holding the three-edged knife crimson with Patel's blood jabbered nervously. The other assassins reverted to familiar native behavior, shoving each other in their haste to scramble out the open window through which they'd entered.

Sick with horror, he let his eyes come back to the DepCom's lifeless body, glazed with its own blood. Then he dropped to his knees. Patel's fingers had flickered briefly.

Something clattered to the floor as he knelt. Ignoring it, he cradled the DepCom's bloody head in his lap. Close up, he caught the faint iron smell of the spreading blood.

"Ries," Patel whispered hoarsely. "I must tell you — Mules — Something I just learned —"

"Save your strength, Chan. I'll get help."

Weak fingers scrabbled at his sleeve. "Important. You *must* know this. The Freh —"

Patel's voice stopped. His head lolled back, his eyes stared unseeing into the lingster's own. Then his colorless lips moved soundlessly, and Ries read his last words: "Save my family."

He stared down at the dead man in his arms for a moment longer. Then he laid the head gently back down on the Indian carpet and stood up.

The assassin still stood, knife in hand, gaping stupidly at the result of his treachery. Ries took a step forward, and the alien bolted, scrambling out the window in his turn.

He glanced back one more time at the body, feeding a growing rage. The broken flask lay beside Patel, *zyth* running like a fiery oil slick over his bloody body.

SIX

The family's private apartment was at the end of a long hallway on the third floor. Ries skidded on wooden tile polished slick every morning by grinning Freh houseboys, the same ones — or their friends and neighbors — who now had the blood of Chandra Patel on their hands. Never in the fifteen years the human colony had been on Krishna had the Freh given any indication they could turn into killers.

The fogginess of the hangover he'd experienced earlier came back, clouding his thoughts as the shocking clarity of Patel's murder faded. He could use a drink — but he knew he had to stay sober now.

The DepCom's bedroom door stood ajar, and he heard the *skreek* of trunks being dragged across the wooden floor, the *thud* and *thump* of the family's frantic packing. He knocked once to announce his presence then went inside without waiting for a reply.

Three-year-old Jilan, the Patels' late-in-life child, sat in a heap of vivid scarlet and turquoise pillows on the huge bed, silently clutching a stuffed toy. He'd always thought there was something fey about this child who'd been born on Krishna. The older daughter was adding her weight to her mother's as they tried to close an overstuffed traveling chest. Lita's eyes were deep brown flecked with gold, and when she'd finished growing out of her awkward years he imagined she'd be as exotic as a tiger. For now, she was a moody teenager, unpredictable as a cat.

"Danyo." Nayana Patel looked up and spotted him. "I can't find a boy to help us. Give me a hand with this."

"Respect, Mem, but we have to get out now. Leave it."

She stared at him, fussing absently at the long, elaborately pleated gown. "I can't go without —"

He grabbed the woman's elbow and turned her toward the door.

The younger daughter wailed. But the older daughter snatched at his sleeve, and he saw scarlet, long-nailed fingers.

"Don't touch my mother!" the girl ordered.

He removed her hands from his sleeve. "We don't have time to waste."

Mem Patel's eyes widened as she caught sight of the blood on his hands where her husband's head had rested. "Chandra?" she whispered. Color drained out of her dark face leaving it grey.

He was afraid she'd break down helplessly if he gave her the truth. But she obviously guessed the news was dire. She clapped a heavily ringed hand over her mouth stifling her exclamation. Then she turned back to the bed, bracelets tinkling, and swept her younger child up. The toddler whimpered as the stuffed toy fell out of her arms. The big case she'd been packing forgotten now, the woman moved to the door.

Lita scowled, pushing a loose strand of copper hair back up on her head. He watched her grab up a smaller case that had been on the floor by the bed, feeling the heat of her dislike. "*What are you, Danyo?*" she'd once asked. "*Monk or fairy? Do you ever even look at women?*" How close she'd come to the truth; since his wife's death, he hadn't been with a woman.

Lita followed her mother to the door.

"Wait." He stepped in front of Mem Patel and looked cautiously around the open door.

The upstairs hallway was deserted, the great house silent, giving no hint of the carnage he'd witnessed downstairs. A sense of wrongness suffused the place. The stairwell leading up to the rooftop was at the opposite end of the hallway from the main staircase. No rooms opened off the hall at this point, no balconies or even windows that opened, and if they were challenged here they'd be cornered.

As the fugitives moved down the hall, a row of holo-portraits of former Deputy Commissioners watched grim-faced, white-robed men and women in ceremonial saris, whose most serious threat during their tenure on Krishna had been the upholding of Hindu customs in the face of Freh indifference and incompetence. To make eye contact with any one of them was enough to activate circuits that would deliver snippets of wisdom in the subject's voice. Some had chosen favorite axioms of diplomacy, others repeated cherished lines from the *Bhagavad Gita*. He didn't look at them. There was no advice modern or archaic they could give him; not one of them had faced a nightmare like this.

"You might not want to tell Mama the truth, Danyo," Lita's low voice said just behind him. "But you'd better soon tell *me* or I'm not going anywhere with you."

He glanced back at the girl's sullen face. "You don't have much of a choice."

"Pah! Your breath stinks of liquor," she said.

Jilan wailed and Mem Patel smothered her child's face against her own breast, muffling the sound. The woman's eyes glittered with tears, but she held her grief in silence. He shepherded the family along until they reached a door that led to the roof stairs. Opening it cautiously, he listened for sounds.

They were directly above a small, walled garden the Patels used for meditation, with a holo-statue of Krishna in a niche surrounded by flowers. It struck him then how the Patels clung to the things of home, how little they'd adjusted to this new life. Yet in this they were no different from the rest of New Bombay colony.

A damp wind was picking up, soughing through the trees on the other side of the wall. Tall and skinny, they reached as high as the flat roof of the Residence. The Freh called the trees "Spirit-Trap," the name serving to suggest again how little he really understood of the Freh or their language. The air was heavy with the clotted green smell of the coming monsoon. His sinuses tingled.

He stepped cautiously outside. Beyond the trees, he saw the other wall, the one that shut New Bombay off from the native town squatting at its feet like a scruffy beggar, and south of the town, Separation River. To the north and east was a great chain of mountains dropping down to foothills in the northwest where it was possible to cross to the rolling sweep of grasslands where the starship was based. Their only hope lay in the safety of the *Star of Calcutta's* base.

The DepCom's silver skipcar crouched on a bullseye pad in the center of the roof, an oversized mosquito about to launch itself into the sky. It was small enough that Mem Patel's luggage, if he'd let her bring it, would've made it unbearably crowded. He didn't need to know much about flying; the onboard AI would take care of most of it. The sooner they embarked the better. He beckoned to the women.

His way was suddenly blocked by a Freh in a voluminous ankle-length, orange-brown garment. A white silk scarf, like all the natives wore during the season of blowing spores, covered his face.

"Talker. Wait," the alien said in Frehti. "No harm."

Mem Patel gasped, but if the mother was scared, the wildcat daughter certainly wasn't.

"Go from our way," Lita said in a high-pitched Frehti that Ries hadn't known she could speak.

The Freh stepped back a pace and allowed the white scarf to slide down, revealing sallow features and one lone tattoo squiggle that began on his forehead and ran down over one cheek. Ries recognized the male alien who'd been in the tavern last night; his name was Born-Bent. The Freh's spine seemed twisted out of alignment, raising one shoulder higher than the other and throwing the head off balance. One eye was dull amber, the other grey. *"What they'd call back home a sport,"* the DepCom had once commented, coming upon the malformed alien in the marketplace.

"What are you doing here?" Ries demanded in Frehti.

Born-Bent had done small services for him from time to time, but he'd never trusted the Freh.

Behind him, he heard the child's voice start up again in a rising whine of protest, and the mother's urgent hushing.

The Freh made a half-servile, half-nervous gesture with his head. "Danger here."

He became aware of the tremor in his hands and shut his fists to still it. "What do you want with me?"

The lipless mouth pulled up in an ugly caricature of a grin. "I do service. Then Talker do service."

He wondered suddenly if the name the aliens called him indicated respect or contempt. Probably the latter, since males didn't seem to hold conversations.

"What service?"

At that point, the little girl screeched loudly.

"What is it, precious one?" Mem Patel asked anxiously.

Born-Bent reached into his tentlike robe with his bandaged hand and pulled something out. "Take."

His hand rose instinctively to ward off attack before he saw what it was the alien held out: the sitar he'd left in the tavern. The cracked gourd that had formed the instrument's resonator at its base had been replaced with the shell of a large, native nut.

"This also."

Ries looked down at a second object the alien laid in his palm. It seemed to be a small bone from an animal with some kind of marks scratched on its surface; at first glance, they resembled the scrawl of the primitive counting system used by the merchants in the bazaar. Yet as he gazed at the bone, something stirred in him, some sense of mystery.

"What is it?"

"Soul bone. Give to the mothers."

He had to raise his own voice over the sound of the child's wailing. "What mothers? Where?"

"Beneath the bones. Go. Great danger."

The last thing he had time to do was carry a native relic to an alien graveyard. Ries shoved the bone into a pocket and looped the carry-cord of the sitar over his shoulder.

He turned back to Lita "Get in the 'car."

"I don't take orders from servants."

"Lita!" Mem Patel scolded.

"Well — he is."

"Your Papa wishes us to go with Danyo, and so we will."

The girl scowled but turned toward the vehicle. He took the still shrieking, red-faced child from her mother. Jilan pummeled his arms with her fists.

Mem Patel suddenly seemed to understand the cause of her child's distress. "Where is it, sweetheart? Tell Mama."

Jilan pointed back toward the open door at the top of the narrow stairwell.

His skin prickled. For a moment he thought he'd heard the rumble of voices rising up the stairwell, the echo of tramping feet. He listened. Nothing.

"We have to leave, Mem. Now!"

The older girl was already in the skipcar; she leaned back out the door, holding her arms out to take her sister. He lifted the child up to Lita's waiting arms, then turned to help the DepCom's widow.

Nayana Patel was running back toward the stairwell door to fetch the child's toy, one hand clutching the ridiculously ornate skirt above her knees. Lita screamed. He lunged after Mem Patel, but Born-Bent grabbed him, pinning his arms. The Freh was surprisingly strong for his small size.

"Talker!" the alien said urgently. "You understand how words make."

As Nayana Patel reached the door, another alien appeared, his body naked but his face scarved in white. Ries caught the prismatic glint of a three-sided knife. Mem Patel screamed, the sound dwindling away into a gurgle as bright red arterial blood spurted high, hitting the lintel as she fell.

"Mama!" Lita wailed.

Two more Freh spilled out onto the roof, stepping carelessly over the downed woman.

He threw his weight against the sport. His head spun dizzily, but he caught Born-Bent off balance and almost broke free.

Born-Bent punched him full in the stomach.

His knees buckled under him and air rushed out of his lungs. The alien dragged him across the roof and shoved him like a sack of vegetables through the door of the skipcar. Inside, the child's deafening noise echoed round the confined metal space. His belly scraped painfully over the ridged floor. Lita's long-nailed fingers scrabbled at his arm, pulling him in; her red hair had come loose from the clip, and long curls spilled over her face.

He glanced out the door again, just in time to see Born-Bent go down under the flash of a blade.

SEVEN

The skipcar was flying low over leafy Spirit-Trap treetops glowing olive by storm light. High crests whipped past only centimeters away. Lita Patel sat in the pilot's seat, frowning out the forward port at the horizon, where the grey-green of the jungle met the iron-grey of the clouded sky. She'd had the presence of mind to get the skipcar airborne after Born-Bent shoved Ries aboard.

"Flying too low," he observed. His eyes were raw and his stomach felt bruised.

"Glad you're feeling better."

"Onboard AI —"

"Overrode it. I'm keeping us under the storm clouds."

He squinted at the jungle flowing like a dark river beneath them. "Didn't know you knew anything about flying."

"More than you, apparently." She turned to look at him. "You drink too much."

In the watery light he saw smudges under her eyes, which were bloodshot as if she'd been crying. Her red hair had come completely loose now, tumbling over her shoulders.

And suddenly he knew that one of the things about her that irritated him so much was that her hair was the same rich color as his young wife's had been. Looking at this half-grown vixen triggered painful memories of his lost, sweet Yv. The sooner they reached the base and he could hand these two over to somebody else the better.

His head felt as if it had been hollowed out; the sound of his own voice when he spoke boomed and echoed inside his skull. He leaned forward and punched up the 'car's automap and studied it. The terrain between New Bombay and the base was hilly and wild; their route passed over a ridge thick with unbroken jungle, a tapestry in vermilion and umber.

"Danyo, I expect you to explain —"

"Not now."

"Then advise me. I've been trying to raise *Calcutta*'s base, but I get no response."

Even with the starship gone, there should be a skeleton maintenance crew left behind. He deactivated the map. "Try again."

She leaned forward and keyed a command into the pad. Nothing happened. "Why don't they answer? Is something wrong?"

He considered possibilities but decided not to share them. Ahead, a jagged spike of lightning streaked out of the black clouds and raced to the ground.

After a moment, she said in a whisper which couldn't hide the shakiness of her voice, "Tell me the truth now, Danyo. My father's dead too, isn't he?"

If they were going to have any chance of getting through this, she would have to grow up. There was no way he could make it painless. "The Freh killed him."

She closed her eyes, and he saw her small white teeth biting her lower lip. She had her mother's ability to absorb terrible news and not cry out. He couldn't remember the death of his own parents — he'd already been on assignment for the Guild — but he knew it wasn't under terrible circumstances like these. He felt there was something he ought to say to her but couldn't think of anything appropriate.

They skimmed over the wind-churned treetops in silence again for a few seconds. Rain spattered in a crazy staccato on the forward port. They'd be lucky to make it to the base before the storm caught them.

Finally, he said lamely, "I'm sorry."

She stared resolutely ahead. "We have to get to the *Calcutta* now."

He hadn't been able to weep after Yv's death. Like Lita, he'd found no time for grief. Instead, he'd taken the way past the pain of living through a bottle of whatever a planet offered. But that had been just another kind of lie.

"The ship isn't at the base right now."

"Not there? Then —"

She didn't get to finish her thought. The little skipcar shuddered as if hit by a giant fist, rolled tail over nose, and headed straight down for the forest floor.

EIGHT

When he opened his eyes again, he was dangling upside down from the seat webbing, the floor of the skipcar above his head. Branches poked their way in through broken ports. A long jagged spike of what was supposed to be shatterproof plastiglass was poised above his neck. It took him a moment to figure out that the 'car must have been caught in a tree that had broken their fall.

What the hell're we going to do now?

The silence made him nervous. Supporting his weight with one hand on a strut, he wriggled cautiously round until the glass no longer threatened to impale him. Now he could see the pilot's seat.

Empty.

He craved a shot of *zyth* to steady his nerves, but he knew he was going to have to do this alone from now on. The thought scared him. Then he abandoned caution and twisted in the web until he could see the back. Also empty. If they'd been ejected —

"You're conscious," Lita said leaning in the window, careless of the splintered glass.

He stared upside down at her. "I thought you might've been killed."

"You don't have that much luck, Danyo." Her expression, wan beneath the coffee-brown skin, gave the lie to the bravado of her words.

"We must've been struck by lightning." He wondered if the onboard AI had been badly damaged, and if it contained a self-repair program.

"I got Jilan out first in case the 'car burned."

She indicated where her sister sat, finger in her mouth, at the foot of a tangle of slender jungle trees. Long emerald fronds dripped rainwater on her.

He noticed that Lita had removed the ornate overskirt she'd been wearing at home — the thought brought back an unwelcome image of Mem Patel's skirt spattered in blood — revealing sturdy brown legs in serviceable shorts. She carried the skirt slung over one shoulder like a cloak. The little strap sandals on her feet were not so practical.

His seat web was jammed and it took time to free himself. Lita helped, supporting him to take tension off the web's fastening.

"Devi! You weigh too much," she grumbled.

He turned, allowing his legs to slide slowly down to the ceiling that was now the floor, and felt the sitar bump against his head. For a moment he considered leaving it behind. But it had been Patel's, and Born-Bent had gone out of his way to mend it and bring it back. It really didn't weigh that much. The sitar's carry-cord had caught in the seat web and had to be untangled. A lightweight jacket he'd thrown into his pack had snagged on the cord too, and came with it.

He rolled himself cautiously out of the wrecked 'car and stood beside the girl in the wet forest. Immediately, his sensitive sinuses tingled painfully.

"Jilan's hungry," Lita said. "She hasn't eaten since —"

He felt heat on the back of his neck and turned to see the skipcar burning. He stared at it for a moment. The forest was too damp for the fire to become a threat, but he hadn't had time to get their belongings out.

"You see?" she said. "Now what?"

Krishna wasn't a world that invited tourism. He knew few things about the foothills other than they were wild and dotted with small Freh villages where some of the bazaar's vendors lived. He'd trusted the skipcar's AI to get them to the base without knowing exactly where it was. Now he was certain of only one thing: They dared not stay here in the jungle, so close to the chaos in New Bombay.

"Now we go on foot," he said.

Lita scuffed a toe in the grass that formed a thick, waist-high carpet under the trees, and drops of water flew off the stalks. "Not much of a path. And what about Jilan? This is over her head."

He glanced in the direction she indicated and saw the little girl pushing her way through grass that reached her shoulders. As he watched, she stumbled and fell, disappearing under a green wave that closed over her. If she went off on her own, they could easily lose track of her.

"I'll carry Jilan."

"Do you know what direction we should take?"

He didn't, but he wasn't going to admit that. Spirit-Trap trees hid the mountains from sight, and the sky was too overcast for him to get his bearings from the sun. If he climbed one of the trees, he'd get a better sense of which way to go, but these trees were too thin to take his weight. He had no idea how many hours had passed since they'd fled New Bombay. He had to do it soon, or what little daylight was left would be fading.

He picked up the toddler and settled her on his shoulders where she twined her fingers in his hair, leaning her head drowsily against his. She was heavy, but at least she'd given up that awful screaming. He wasn't used to children, and he'd never had much contact with this one in New Bombay; she'd stayed most of the time in the nursery with the family's personal servants.

"Be careful with my sister," Lita warned. "She's very upset."

He glanced at the older girl. It wasn't the first time he'd noticed her interpreting for her silent sibling. "Doesn't she speak for herself?"

"Why should she? My mother spoiled her. And the amahs did everything for her. Everybody around her did the talking."

Three was late for a child to begin talking, he thought. All healthy human babies were born with impressive linguistic skills. Jilan should be conveying her thoughts with some fluency by now, not relying on others to do it for her.

Somewhere a stream rushed by, hidden in the dense undergrowth, chattering urgently to itself. The sharp, clear scent of water lay like a descant over the darker notes of wet soil and thick plant life. Enormous magenta and scarlet blossoms hung from vines that climbed the tree trunks; smaller, acid yellow flowers lit up the shadows beneath them. Clouds of eyeless insects whirred by; guided only by the smell of the flowers, they blundered constantly into the humans' faces. He pushed his way through the high grass and Lita followed.

"These sandals are rubbing my feet," she complained at one point.

He wouldn't have believed the brutal carnage they'd left behind in the Residence was the work of Freh if he hadn't seen them himself. Something had caused the normally placid aliens to rise up against the humans. If they'd been harboring deep resentment against the colonists all these years, they'd done a good job of hiding it. He tried to remember if he'd ever sensed anger or even reluctance in the native behavior, but all the images he conjured up were of bland, incurious, passive faces.

"You understand how words make." Born-Bent had been wrong; he didn't understand at all. There were obviously huge gaps in his knowledge of how Frehti operated. He wished he could take the problem back to the Guild, let his old teachers play with it. He imagined them as he'd known them in his youth. Magistra Eiluned, old already when he'd first come to the Mother House, and Dom Houston, who'd believed that every language served only to disguise. Was Frehti disguising something he should know? In memory he saw them gathered round the seminar table while the warm green smell of summer flowed through tall windows, and cuckoos spoke from sunlit apple orchards.

A stifled exclamation at his side brought him back. Lita had caught one of her flimsy sandals in a wiry grass strand. He put out a hand and steadied her.

When the sandal was settled back on her foot, she glanced up at him. "Do you have any idea what caused that . . . that . . . what happened back there?"

Her voice wavered, but he could tell she was determined not to let him see her terror. Hair in disarray, clothing streaked and torn, she was, after all, hardly out of childhood herself.

"Time to talk about it later," he said.

Something had happened in the native tavern. Born-Bent had tried to give him a message and perhaps been killed for it. The DepCom had tried to share something he'd learned. Again, something important enough for a man to waste his dying breath trying to communicate. Ries had a sense of huge pieces of information lacking, questions without answers. Until he understood the deadly puzzle, he and the DepCom's children were in mortal danger.

NINE

When they'd gone a few hundred meters through the dense undergrowth, he found what he was looking for. An old Spirit-Trap with a thick, gnarled trunk shoved its head up through the canopy formed by its younger neighbors. He let the child and the sitar slide gently down to the wet grass. Jilan clung to his leg for a moment, staring up at him wide-eyed, but she made no sound. He was beginning to find the child's silence unnerving.

"Wait here a minute," he said. "Okay?"

Jilan didn't answer.

"What're you doing now?" Lita asked as he began to climb. She seemed to have pulled herself together again. "You'll never make that, Danyo. You're out of shape."

The smooth trunk was slick from the rain but free of the clinging vines. Near the top, the main trunk split into three, and he could go no further as each thin limb bent under his weight. He sat in the security of this three-pronged Y, blood pounding in his temples, leaning out precariously to gaze over the surrounding forest.

The rain had stopped and the sun had already set, leaving a diffuse glow in the banked clouds on the horizon. To his left, the storm had cleared, and he saw the first faint spark of the constellation the Freh called "The Thief." Below it, a white smear, a tail end of the home galaxy that the Freh knew as "Sorrow-Crossing" gleamed faintly. Somewhere down that soft wash of light, a small blue planet orbited a sun too insignificant to be visible this far away.

He looked away. Fugitives couldn't afford the luxury of being homesick.

They were on the slope of one of the foothills, a gentle rise that he hadn't noticed as they'd trudged through the thick jungle. He gazed across canyons choked with dark vegetation and saw Separation River, glowing like a pewter ribbon in the twilight, winding across the alluvial plain. He thought of his first impressions of Krishna as the shuttle ferrying him down from the starship came in through the atmosphere: A lush green planet laced with shining waterways, signs of squalid habitation appearing only after the shuttle landed.

In the foreground, downslope, he noticed a number of trees seemed to be leaning crazily, and he realized he was staring at the skipcar's crash site. Then his attention was pulled back to the distant human settlement on the banks of the river. It seemed as if it were illuminated. As he stared, it erupted in a fountain of flame that turned the bluffs crimson. New Bombay was on fire.

"How much longer are you going to stay up there?"

It was completely dark on the forest floor when he slid back down the tree again, but his eyes retained the afterimage of flame. The DepCom had thought danger would come from the wild Mules, yet it was the placid Freh who'd rebelled, and that was more frightening.

"Well, did you find which way we have to go?"

"I think so."

No sense passing on to her what he'd learned from the AI of carnivores on Krishna. As if to underline his concern, the leathery black shape of a huge nightbird slipped between the trees and swept past his shoulder. He heard the slap and creak of its featherless wings.

And he heard something else. Something more menacing than a wild animal.

"What? Danyo, why're you pushing me?"

"Up there." He jerked his chin at the tree he'd just climbed down. "We'll wait up there till it's light."

"But I don't climb trees. And what about Jilan?"

He shoved the hesitating girl toward the tree. "Get your foot up on that bole there. Then the other. Keep going!" He slung the sitar over his shoulder, grabbed the child up and held her close to his chest with one hand, reaching into the tree's darkness for a handhold with the other. The fieldpack dug into his hip as the child clasped her legs around him.

Lita seemed to pick up his urgency and she climbed quickly. He followed, burdened by the child and the sitar that he couldn't leave behind in the damp grass. It banged into his shoulder blades with each movement. Scared by the ascent, the little girl made it worse by clinging tightly to his hair. Lita's foot slipped twice on the damp trunk and struck his fingers, almost knocking him off. The child struggled, and he had a hard time hanging on to the slippery bark.

"Stay calm!" he commanded.

She whimpered but stopped struggling. Lita had now reached the Y where he'd stopped earlier; he pushed the child up into her down-stretched hands. Relieved of Jilan's weight, he scrambled up after her.

He heard the harsh intake of Lita's breath as she turned toward the plain of Separation River. The entire sky to the south and east was lit by the lurid glow of the fire, and under it the wet leaves of the forest canopy glittered redly as if they'd been drenched in blood.

Below them, the forest suddenly filled with screams — the crash of bodies running blindly through undergrowth — a high-pitched keening that brought the hairs up on his neck and arms. A sudden smell like putrefying flesh rose up to his nostrils.

"Merciful Lord Krishna!" Lita exclaimed, her hands clasped over her nose. "What is it?"

At the foot of the tree that sheltered them, a naked, spindlylegged creature, its corpse-white skin hanging in folds like a too-big overcoat hastily thrown over spikes of underlying bone, wrestled a plump Freh female to the ground. The Freh shrieked and thrashed about as the other alien covered her. Ries could see her fists pummeling the larger alien's shoulders — a male, he could see its elongated penis and scrotal sack — and he heard the stream of scolding she gave vent to in her birdlike voice. The male made no sound in reply.

This was the first Mule he'd ever seen close up, and he was stunned by the height and emaciation of the alien. The powerful reek of their violent mating rose up in a thick cloud till he thought he would vomit.

Then it was over. The Mule stood up, his long, horselike head turning slowly, the overlarge ears pricked as if they were listening to sounds out of human range. Then he vanished wraithlike into the trees. A moment later, the Freh female picked herself up from the ground, brushed leaves and dirt off, then strolled away as if nothing had happened.

It made no sense. The Freh and the Mules were separate species; that was obvious at a glance. Had he misunderstood what was happening?

Lita was crying now. The mask of arrogance and precociousness that marked the teenager in the bazaar this morning had dropped away. The younger daughter stared up at him, her eyes wide with fright, her hands gripping the front of his jumpsuit.

"She looked like one of Jilan's amahs," Lita said in a wobbly voice. "What're we going to do, Danyo?"

"We'll stay up here for the night. In the morning, we'll make plans."

He put one arm around each of them, drew them close to share a little warmth, and thought about what she'd just said. The girl obviously didn't share her mother's boast that she couldn't tell one Freh from another.

The lurid glow in the sky over New Bombay gradually faded. The storm had blown over for the time being, leaving a sky bright with alien constellations and the white trail of Sorrow-Crossing. The planet had no companion in its orbit round its sun; Krishna's night sky was perpetually moonless. He looked down. Now the wet leaves mirrored the fierce glitter of stars.

When it was light again in the morning, he'd try to remember information browsed in the computer's library about edible plants and roots. One protein-rich, red-brown tuber the natives roasted over hot coals, he'd tasted in the bazaar. The Freh used the husks to make the dye they favored for their own robes. If he could find some tomorrow it would solve the food problem.

Something dug into his ribs where the child clung to him. He took Born-Bent's soul bone out and examined it curiously. It was about the size and width of his own index finger, and in the starlight its surface gleamed almost as though it were translucent. He ran his finger over the symbol scratched on it, but it yielded no secrets to him. The mothers — whoever and wherever they were — would know what to do with it, the Freh had said. If he survived long enough to find them.

After a while, the girls slept, but he remained awake and watchful for a long time, listening to the sounds of flight and evasion and bestial rutting that came from all directions, punctuated with an ominous animal roaring that brought to mind the chilling sights and sounds of jungle life he'd found in the AI's library.

TEN

He slept fitfully. Shortly before dawn, he dreamed Yv was drowning in Separation River. She was wearing the sky blue dress she'd worn on their wedding day, and her outstretched hands implored him to help while he stood on the other bank, unable to reach her.

When he woke, his head had the sticky, cobweb-filled feeling he knew well, a clogged dullness that *zyth* caused and only *zyth* could remove.

His muscles jumped and trembled this morning. Fire raced down the nerve paths, and sweat broke out on his brow in spite of the cool morning. He felt weak, drained, ready to give up, desperate for the courage *zyth* could give him, even if it didn't last.

The forest had dissolved in a pearl-white mist that dripped off the leaves. He looked down at Jilan, still nestled in the crook of his arm. She was awake, gazing up at him, thumb in mouth, her face puffy and tear-streaked. *This wasn't part of my Guild oath.* But for the child's sake, he had to pull himself together.

Lita was kneeling in the tall grass in the grey light, emptying something out of her skirt which she'd used as a basket. Wisps of fog drifted slowly over the ground.

She glanced up at him. "I found breakfast while you were still snoring."

He wouldn't give her the satisfaction of seeing her barbs strike home. He let the sitar slide down until it was low enough to drop safely into her outstretched hands. Then he grasped Jilan with one shaky hand and with the other lowered himself down to stand beside Lita. The little girl wriggled free and clutched her sister's arm. Lita pulled her sister down to sit on the ground close beside her, then indicated a mound of thumbnail-sized, dark purple berries.

"The houseboys sometimes brought us berries," she said. "They looked a bit like these."

He picked one out of the mound and raised it cautiously to his nose, then broke the berry open with a fingernail and gazed at the honeycomb of tiny segments surrounding a small oval seed. "This one's okay."

He handed it to her and picked up another.

"You mean you're going to do that with each one?" she asked, her disbelief obvious. "But they all came from the same bush. If one's okay —"

"Three kinds of berries all grow on one bush. They all look alike on the outside. The one I gave you is female, safe to eat. Another kind contains the male chromosomes, a kind of red dust that will make you sneeze and your stomach cramp, but it won't kill you. The third is sexually neuter. It's designed to kill the plant's enemies that mistake it for one of the other two."

She clapped her hands over her mouth. "But I was so hungry, and they looked — Danyo, I already ate one."

"Does your stomach hurt?"

She shook her head.

"You were lucky. Next time, wait for me."

"I was only trying to help," she said in a small voice.

He sat cross-legged on the wet ground and sniffed, split and sorted the berries, discarding most of them, stopping to sneeze frequently. Both sisters watched him work. Finally he took a berry from the smallest pile and — to reassure Lita — put it with great show into his own mouth. Then he turned that pile over to her.

"Those you can eat safely."

"You're only going to eat one berry?"

"I'm not hungry."

He didn't tell her that *zyth* was distilled from the poisonous form of these berries, made safe only after a long period of fermentation, and perhaps not even then. Hunger for *zyth* rose up from his bowels like a starved beast, all claws and teeth, overwhelming his body's need for food. For a moment he considered saving the dangerous berries. If he put one under his tongue, sucked it, didn't chew —

He stood up abruptly and walked away from temptation.

While the children ate their meager breakfast, the sun rose and the mist gradually melted off the grass. A fallen tree trunk provided a place to sit. He unslung the sitar from his shoulder, settled it in his lap, and began to explore the strings with a hand that wouldn't stop trembling. The native nut that had replaced the cracked gourd changed the resonance, and he compensated for it as much as he could. He really needed a wire plectrum to pluck the strings, but that hadn't been in his pocket when Born-Bent returned the lost instrument to him.

His fingernails were still caked in the DepCom's blood. He wiped his hand clean in the wet grass.

Lita came over to sit beside him as he finished. Her red hair tangled over her shoulders, and pink juice from the berries stained her mouth. Jilan was drawing on a patch of bare ground, using a piece of dry grass she'd pulled from the forest floor. Absorbed by her work, the child paid no attention to them. The two looked nothing alike, he thought. Lita would be as voluptuous as her mother but taller when she matured; the child was elfin-faced and seemed destined to be small and delicate.

"That was my father's sitar," Lita said.

"Yes."

"Play something."

He picked out an old song he'd learned as a student, a lament for time past and homeland lost, like a thousand similar dirges sung in different languages over the millennia by humans who'd been explorers and wanderers since they emerged from the primal ocean.

"Sad. It reminds me of Earth."

He set the instrument down on the ground beside him.

"I never learned to play. I think it would've pleased my father if I had." She ran one finger tip down the length of a string. "I've been away so long, it's hard to remember Earth let alone India. Have you ever been to India?"

He shook his head and stood up, working on tension in his neck and shoulders.

"One thing I remember is a white house in the mountains, near the headwaters of the Ganges. We lived there in the summertime. We had peacocks and monkeys in the gardens —"

She broke off. He watched her staring into the distance, the rising sun illuminating half her face, highlighting the dark cheekbones so that she seemed a bas-relief carving of a young goddess on a temple wall.

In the silence, he bent down and retrieved the sitar, sliding an arm through its carry-cord. "Time to move on."

After a while she said, "You must've met lots of aliens."

"A number. They're not all pleased to meet Homo sapiens."

She scrambled to her feet and took her sister's hand. They stepped out through tough, wiry grass that grew up to the height of the child's head. He took Jilan from Lita and swung her up onto his shoulders. The child grasped the neck of the sitar as she rode, which didn't prevent it from banging his back but tightened the carry-cord as it passed across his throat.

Lita walked beside him. "How did you know about the berries?"

"There was a wealth of information in the AI's library. Your father seemed to be the only person in New Bombay who was interested in it."

She was silent for a moment, then she said, "You don't like me very much, do you?"

"Not important. I have to get you to safety."

"Well, maybe it's mutual." She halted, staring at the stark peaks, bones shrouded in funeral grey mist. "I hate this planet. Especially those ugly mountains."

He glanced up without slowing his pace. "The Maker's Bones?"

She caught up with him again. "And why do they have that name? Do the Freh believe in a god called the Maker? Is he supposed to be buried up there or what?"

"I haven't seen any evidence the Freh have a god."

"How can that be? All primitive species have gods or goddesses."

Before he could answer, something crashed through the undergrowth ahead of them. He seized Lita's arm and pulled them all down behind a tall clump of the bushes. Jilan whimpered and pressed her face against his chest.

The noise grew closer, and now they could hear snuffling — growling — keening —

"What is it?" Lita whispered, her breath warm at his ear.

Three figures emerged from the trees, a tall Mule male with deep-set eyes and two male Freh, one a juvenile, wrapped in rags and still showing the distinctive rolls of adolescent neck fat. The Mule tackled the naked adult Freh and wrestled him to the ground. They rolled over and over in the grass, the Mule grunting, the Freh screeching, and both pounding each other, at one point coming so dangerously close to the humans' hiding place that Ries smelled the Freh's sour sweat and the rancid odor of the Mule.

The Mule appeared to be trying to sink long fangs into the Freh's arms while the juvenile stood by, shrilling and gesturing with his four-fingered hands. Ries would never have guessed from the starved look of the Mule that he would be so strong, but he was obviously getting the better of the sturdier-looking Freh.

As abruptly as the sexual encounter had ended last night, this fight ended. Now the combatants separated, not looking at each other, sat up and brushed dirt off themselves. A long moment passed. When he finally stood, the Mule's thin arms were as long as his legs; Ries saw the bones clearly through the skin as if the alien were a walking anatomy demonstration.

The Freh turned unblinking eyes in the direction of the hidden humans, but far from signaling defeat, there was something that seemed glutted and satisfied in that expression. There was some unexplained connection here, some clue he was missing that would explain the bizarre interaction between these two species that he'd witnessed last night and today, but he had no idea what it could be.

Through all this, the juvenile continued to wail. Suddenly, the Mule seemed to become aware of the noise for the first time. With a roar that was almost too deep to come from such a sunken chest, he now turned on the younger Freh. At first Ries thought he meant to kill the juvenile, but he saw that the Mule's intention was to drive him away. The juvenile took a step back, his eyes large with fear, arms flapping ineffectually in front of his face. The Mule lunged forward.

Then, to Ries's astonishment, the adult Freh joined the chase. At this, the juvenile turned and ran. The Mule and the adult Freh both ran after him. The sounds of the chase gradually died away behind them and the silence of the forest returned. Ries blew breath out, releasing tension.

"I want to go home!" Lita clutched her little sister.

He sighed. "New Bombay burned last night. You saw the fire."

"Not New Bombay. Earth."

He didn't think any of them had much chance of ever seeing Earth again.

ELEVEN

Warm rain pelted them without ceasing, and sodden blind bugs crashed against their faces and hands. He'd given his light jacket to Lita who was carrying her sister on her back; both of them huddled under it. Their hair hung limp and wet over faces streaked with mud. Lita's flimsy sandals had disintegrated in the rain, and now she wore his boots, lashed around her ankles with vines to prevent them falling off. His own feet were protected only by socks with strips of tree bark to fortify the soles, also secured with vines; leaves jiggled festively as they walked. The tropical white jumpsuit he'd put on yesterday morning was now filthy and ripped.

Lita seemed in better spirits this morning. He heard her murmuring to her sister, telling her how close they were to the *Calcutta's* base, how soon they'd be there. Maybe he'd had the same optimistic resiliency when he was her age; he certainly didn't now. He trudged, head down, water pouring down his back. His empty stomach protested constantly and his tired muscles ached. His nerves shivered with need, and it was hard to stop thinking about *zyth*. One shot of it would be like grabbing power lines in his bare hands, electricity racing across the connection, burning, energizing.

It would be so much easier to give up, lie down, surrender —

I am a channel...Through me flows the meaning of the Universe...

The words of the lingster's mantra rose unbidden in his mind, dragging him back from the abyss. *First was the Word and I am its carrier.*

He had to go on. There was no choice; the Guild had seen to that. The Guild had branded him, and there was no removing the mark from his soul. Alien alcohol was his attempt to break the bond and it had failed, just as it had failed to take away the pain of Yv's death.

He swatted insects and moved on. He was glad for the small relief of being rid of the younger child for a while, and not just because of the burden of carrying her extra weight on his back. Jilan's continuing silence was unnerving. She didn't respond to anything he said to her. He had no idea what to do about her.

If Yv had lived, he wondered, would she have wanted children? One of them would've had to leave the Guild since the Guild discouraged childraising by its lingsters. Would she have done so gladly? Could he have accepted her decision, whatever it might've been? A memory surfaced: She lay under him in a grove of giant, singing ferns on an exotic world, the first time they'd made love; the wild red hair spilled over her small, firm breasts, her eyes in shadow the color of moss, a sprinkling of rosy freckles over her nose. He ached to realize there were things about his young wife he hadn't had time to learn.

Underneath his thoughts, like an evil mantra, the need for *zyth* pulsed. He should've gathered the berries. He could go back — just a small detour — It took all his fading strength to prevent his feet from leaving the path and turning back.

First was the Word...

The depth of his need for *zyth* terrified him. He had to escape this nightmare addiction before it was too late, and abstinence was the only way to free himself.

The jungle gave way slowly to the sparser vegetation of the hill country; trees were not so towering here, their leaves sprouting higher up the trunk. And the grass no longer grew so tall.

They heard it first: an insistent murmur like faraway traffic, growing to an animal roar. Then the ground sloped under their feet and they came out suddenly from the forest to stand on a bank where trees tumbled down a ravine to the west. Through the bare branches they glimpsed water, an emerald cascade flashing over the rock face in the subdued light and racing away through the undergrowth. One of the many tributaries of Separation River with its headwaters in the mountain range they were skirting, it lay directly in their path, too wide and flowing much too fast for them to cross.

His mind woozy with fatigue, he stared at it, trying to remember the automap he'd consulted before the skipcar crashed. There shouldn't have been a river that size anywhere near. How had he gone wrong?

"What do we do now?" Lita asked, her voice husky.

It was a fair question. New Bombay was gone. The *Calcutta's* base was probably deserted but better than nothing if he could've been certain he could find his way across this country. Which apparently he couldn't.

Then he thought of something. "You speak Frehti."

A spot of color came and went on her high cheekbones. "Well, I've learned a little."

More than a little, I'll wager, he thought. "Do you remember what the Freh sport said to us as we left the Residence?"

She frowned. "Something about his mother?"

"Not his mother. 'The Mothers.' I think it's a title."

"Well, where do we find them?"

"*Under the bones,*" the misshapen alien had said, and he'd imagined a graveyard of some sort. But now he realized it meant The Maker's Bones, the sharp-toothed mountains to the north. They'd been heading northwest when the skipcar went down, crossing the foothills to get to the base. They needed to change course.

"Northeast and uphill, I think."

"Up *there?*" she asked, her voice full of skepticism.

"Could be our only hope for help."

"Who's to say these 'Mothers' will be friendly? The rest of the natives aren't."

"We don't have a lot of options."

She heaved a deep sigh for his benefit. "How far?"

"Far enough."

He gazed up at the distant peaks. Perhaps a two-day journey on foot, maybe longer because of the child. The rain was bad enough here where the thinning trees still provided some shelter. Up on the ridge, they would be exposed to the full force of monsoon winds and torrential rain and the cold of high altitude at night. It would take all his strength to get them through this, but he had no strength anymore. They needed — deserved — a far better guide.

Lita was right, whether the Mothers would shelter them was doubtful, but he couldn't think of an alternative. And there was nobody else around to help them.

He selected a peak shaped like the broken tooth of a jungle beast as a reference point, then lifted Jilan off her sister's back.

"Let's get moving," he said.

TWELVE

For the next two days they made slow progress over rugged ground, keeping the distinctively shaped peak in sight at all times. The land sloped steeply up through boulders and rocky outcropping; the tall, tropical growth of the jungle floor gave way swiftly to low, wind-battered trees with sharp needles instead of leaves. Cold rain sleeted down all day. The ground beneath their feet turned to mud, slowing their progress further.

"We'll take a break here." He indicated an isolated clump of stunted Spirit-Traps that seemed as lost and out of place as the human fugitives on these high slopes and in almost as much danger of not surviving.

They huddled together in the meager shelter, watching the rain. Lita leaned back against a knobby trunk and closed her eyes; after a while, her regular breathing told him she slept. He needed sleep too, but the constant itch of his craving for *zyth* prevented him from finding it.

Jilan seemed unable to sleep. He studied her. There was nothing dull or retarded about the eyes that gazed back at him, and he knew she wasn't deaf. Then why didn't she talk like a normal three-year-old? He seemed to remember hearing her exploring pre-speech sounds like all human children, trying out the full range available before settling on the ones selected by the language that would become their native tongue and forgetting how to make the others. But she hadn't progressed to the next stage.

"Baby," he said softly, so as not to wake Lita. "Talk to me. Say: 'Ries. Hello, Ries.'"

He sounded ridiculous to himself. It gave him a sudden respect for mothers everywhere who provided models for their children to learn language from. The little girl stared at her hands in her lap.

"Try: 'Hello Lita.'"

Nothing. He pondered for a moment, made another decision.

"*Taq'na,*" he said. Food, in Frehti.

Her dark eyes flicked briefly over him. Not much, but more reaction than he'd got for Inglis. Encouraged, he tried again.

"*Yati.* How about that one? *Yati.* Mama."

She blinked at him and he feared for a moment she was going to cry. *Idiot!* he thought. Why bring up bad memories? But she'd obviously grown bored already; she began to trace patterns in the mud with her fingers. Not surprising that she reacted to Frehti, he decided. She'd probably had more interaction with her alien amahs than she'd had with her parents.

His musings were interrupted by a bout of sneezing. His nose was constantly on fire with invading spores. The DepCom's daughters didn't seem to be as bothered by the phenomenon; Lita sneezed occasionally and rubbed her eyes, Jilan's nose was runny, but neither one was seriously affected. His immune system was challenged more than theirs. The AI had warned about *zyth* addiction's side effects, but he hadn't paid attention, arrogantly certain none of it was ever going to happen to him.

After a while, Lita woke up, and they continued their journey. Along the way, he kept his gaze on the ground, searching for signs of the nutritious tuber that would solve one of their problems, not daring to venture far off the path he'd set for fear of getting them further lost. He didn't find any.

Their second night out, he had better luck and found a sheltered place between a jumble of huge boulders where he could light a small fire to dry their clothes. That night he also found the last of the edible berries for their supper, but not enough for all three. Even with his share added to hers, the child whimpered from hunger, her face wan and pinched with distress.

It wasn't hunger that sent the spasm through his body, and it took all his willpower not to put one of the poison berries under his tongue. *Just one — How could one hurt? — You'd feel so much better* — the seductive voice inside his head pleaded and cajoled. You could handle one.

His hands shook so badly as he handed Lita her share of the berries that she noticed.

"It's *zyth*, isn't it? You need some."

He sat down on the other side of the fire from her. "Who told you that?"

"Mama said you were an incurable drunkard. She said it was a scandal the Guild sent you to us."

"A lot of things your mother never understood."

"She said it was good we didn't have to pay the Guild too much for your services because you were squandering all your share in the native taverns."

"None of her business what I did with my money."

"My father always defended you when they argued, did you know that?"

He felt too sick to be angry. "I don't want to hear any more. Get some rest."

"Well, don't go and die on us during the night, will you?"

She lay down and covered herself and her sister with his jacket and was soon sleeping soundly. He stared at the little fire till the flames flickered out. It took him a long time before anger and need both subsided, allowing him to fall asleep for a little while too.

*****

The third night, they were not so lucky. After a long, exhausting day when at times he despaired of finding a way around the huge boulders in their path while the child cried constantly from hunger, they camped out on stony ground on a windswept ridge where even the thorny bushes couldn't take hold. The rain held off when the sun went down, but it was bitterly cold and he found nothing to burn.

For a long time after Jilan had closed her eyes, he heard the soft muffled sound of Lita weeping. After the girl finally fell asleep, he sat stiffly beside them, every muscle in his body aching from physical exertion, his nerves vibrating with a desperate craving for *zyth* that wouldn't let him sleep.

It was time he faced the truth. He didn't know these mountains. He had no clear idea where he was going. He was incapable of looking after himself; how could he hope to take care of these two children? Only a fool would take seriously native superstitions about "souls" and "Mothers" who might or might not exist. How could they help him even if they did? He'd made a bad decision. They should've tried to get across the river to the base. There was no way they would survive this ordeal, and just as he felt he'd been indirectly responsible for Yv's death, he would now be to blame for the death of the DepCom's children.

He pulled Born-Bent's bone out of his pocket and peered at the symbol carved on it. Disgusted, he flipped the bone into the darkness. He heard it glance off a rock.

Then he lay down, and immediately distinguished the uncomfortable lump of the fieldpack from the sharp stones digging into his ribs. Even now, he couldn't violate his training and throw the thing away. He hadn't thought so much about the Guild in years, and now he could hardly get it out of his mind. It rode on his heartbeat and slid through his veins; he was as addicted to the Guild as he was to *zyth*. He couldn't lift his hands without its laws springing up in his path. He had never hated the Guild so fiercely nor needed it so much.

He shifted the pack so it wasn't directly beneath him, and closed his eyes. At once, all the useless, stupid, shameful scenes out of his past sprang vividly to his mind. The opportunities the Guild had given him that he'd wasted, his constant failure to live up to the lingster code, the way he'd ultimately betrayed Yv, he relived them all. Dark thoughts skittered through his brain, tormenting him late into the night.

THIRTEEN

He came suddenly awake just before sunup, conscious of someone bending over him. His skin crawled as he forced himself to bear the silent scrutiny without flinching. Whoever it was could've killed him as he slept but hadn't. Beside him, he could feel Jilan's small body, wedged between him and her sister for warmth. Both girls were still sleeping.

He heard a sudden intake of breath above him. Cautiously, he slitted his eyes and looked up.

A pudgy, adult male Freh knelt over him, layered in the familiar ankle-length, orange-brown cloth. The Freh's head was turned, tilted as if he were listening to some sound coming from the direction of the jagged peaks which loomed white as snow this morning in cold predawn light, looking more like the fangs of a beast than bones.

Then the alien became aware the human was awake, and his head swiveled back in alarm. Ries stared at him. One half of the Freh's face was covered with an ugly red blotch that spread from just below the hairline to well below the chin. The nose was twisted and warped off-center, a defect that pulled one eye down with it and trapped the nictitating membrane halfway over the eyeball.

The Freh scrambled to his feet, keening anxiously. Something slipped out of his fingers. Ries sat up. Now he could see that behind the male there was a female gesturing to him.

"What do you want?" he said in Frehti.

At the sound of his voice, Lita woke up. She took one look at the Freh and shrieked. The Freh stumbled away in obvious panic. The female clutched his arm and hobbled beside him, half pulling her companion, half being dragged along by him.

"Devi!" Lita said. "I've never seen such an ugly one."

The native was another sport, only the second he'd seen.

The child was awake and whimpering now. Lita stooped and picked her sister up. "Are we just going to let them get away?"

The two Freh were scrambling up a rocky incline toward the nearest peak. He watched their awkward progress; they seemed to know where they were going. And if they could do it, so could humans.

"No. We're going to follow them."

"Jilan can't go much further without food."

As he bent down to retrieve the sitar, something caught his eye. The bone lay out in the open where the alien had dropped it. He picked it up; a crack obliterated part of the markings. He dropped it back in his pocket.

Lita took two shuffling steps forward with her sister perched on one hip. The girl's exhaustion was apparent in the slump of her shoulders, her pinched expression. He caught up with her and took Jilan from her.

"I'll carry my father's sitar," Lita said.

They stumbled forward silently for a while, no energy left over for talk, while the land rose inexorably beneath their feet.

The rising sun brought no warmth, and the dazzle it struck from the bare peaks hurt his eyes. At least it had stopped raining, and his nose seemed a little less sore. Lita had shut her eyes against the fierce light and walked blindly, clinging to his arm. He squinted through lowered eyelids, his vision narrowed down to the point where he felt as if he were sleepwalking. With his free hand, he adjusted the way the fieldpack rode at his waist. One good thing had come from so much exercise and so little food: his belt fit looser now than it had a few days ago.

Yet in spite of his exhaustion and the pressing need for food, he felt better in spirit than he had in a long time. Miraculously, his mind was clear and pure as spring water this morning. The self-hatred of the night before seemed to have burned away; possibilities spun in the bright air like butterflies in the apple orchards at the Mother House. He looked deep into his being and found it miraculously free of the demon that had bound him for so long. He took a deep breath. He might not have a coherent plan for their survival, but for the first time since Chandra Patel's murder he knew hope.

It was such a ludicrous emotion under the circumstances that he laughed aloud. In the thin air of this high altitude, the laughter soon turned to gasping for breath.

"Come not nearer."

The Frehti words cut short his amusement. Shielding his eyes against the sun with one hand, he peered at the small, bent figure of an old Freh female standing directly in his path.

His heart jumped with the realization: An *old* female.

She wore a long, shapeless brown garment of some coarse, woven material, the hood thrown back from her lined face revealing thin, greying fur on her head. She was holding a three-edged Freh knife ready to strike, reminding him powerfully of Patel's assassins. Belatedly, he set Jilan down, pushing her and Lita behind him.

"Name yourself," the old female said. "Tell what you seek here."

"I am called Ries Danyo. I seek the Mothers."

"You have found. I am called First-Among-Mothers."

The word she used was *Na-freh'm-ya*, and he heard a common root in it, but she didn't give him time to think about it. She gestured with one clawlike hand, and they were suddenly surrounded by three more hooded figures who had come up on his blind side where they'd been hiding in sun dazzle. All three carried the vicious-looking triple-edged knives.

Before he could react, the little girl was taken from his grasp. Seeing one of the hooded figures lifting her sister, Lita yelled and kicked at her own captors. Ries's arms were seized and rapidly bound to his sides; his nose filled with the powdery scent he associated with old age, and something danker, an underground smell that clung to their robes.

Every one of their captors, he saw, was bent, wrinkled, grey-furred, skinny-necked, and female. It would've been funny, he thought, a gang of old alien females struggling uphill with a furious human teenager and a wailing human child, if he could've been sure they wouldn't resort to using those knives.

First-Among-Mothers held up one hand, stopping Lita's noisy protest. "Little one safer here than Danyo."

"Why is Danyo not safe with the Mothers?" he asked.

She stopped abruptly in his path and he almost fell. One of the other females yanked his bonds, pulling him upright. First-Among-Mothers's face was an arm's length away from his. In spite of the situation, he was fascinated by this close view.

There was nothing here of the blandness that had marked every Freh's features he'd seen until now, yet she was no sport. The round, amber eyes, curdled with age till they resembled milky opals, held a depth of intelligence that was unmistakable. He read anger in them, but also a touch of humor in the lines at their edges as if she laughed at herself for a role she was playing. Something in her expression seemed to say this was all an elaborate joke. The effect was so human that he felt convinced he could read her basic goodwill. It was almost impossible not to anthropomorphize and think of her as an old woman.

He knew instantly to distrust his naive reaction. He'd forgotten a lot of the Guild's teachings over the years, and disobeyed more, but this stayed in his mind: The closer to human an alien appeared, the more difficult it was for a human to read its intentions.

"Danyo male," First-Among-Mothers said.

"But Danyo not Freh," he countered.

She considered this for a moment. "No trust here."

At that, they all resumed their uphill journey. The old Freh females urged the humans to hurry with kicks and slaps and the occasional warning prick from the tip of a knife, though he noticed that they were easier on Lita than they were on him.

He felt like Gulliver captured by the Lilliputians.

FOURTEEN

It was past noon when the party halted in the shadow of the broken peak he'd used as a bearing.

"In," First-Among-Mothers said.

The females escorting Lita and Jilan went ahead through a narrow opening in the rock. He did as he was told, and found himself at the top of a flight of steps carved into rock walls. Torchlight made shadows leap on the walls.

"Down."

He went down.

The steps opened up into a cavern, broad and high-ceilinged, with rough-hewn pillars supporting balconies that overhung shadowy side aisles. The stone floor was covered with a layer of rushes, and plainly woven hangings gave privacy to different areas. While it was still cool down here, it was several degrees warmer than the air outside, for which he was grateful. But he was mostly struck by its resemblance to the monastic design of the refectory, the oldest building of the Guild's Mother House. The cavern lacked only modern means of lighting and windows to look out on high mountains rather than be buried beneath them as here. A long wooden table down the center completed the resemblance.

Old females sat together on stone benches in groups of two or three, all wearing the same kind of homespun robes. The scene was almost reassuring in its domesticity, until he noticed the glitter of a knife tucked in one old crone's belt.

They were stared at with a good deal of open-mouthed curiosity, but unlike just about every Freh he'd ever come in contact with, these old females didn't grin in the presence of humans. It was always an odd sensation to be stared at as a human on an alien world, one he'd had many times but never managed to get used to. Suddenly, when he least expected it, the tables would be turned and he'd perceive himself as the alien in the crowd, the man far from home.

From somewhere in the vast cave came the aroma of food being prepared. The smell made his knees buckle with hunger. Now he was pushed back against one of the columns. He resisted and a female slapped him across the mouth, making him taste blood. His thighs encountered a hard edge, and he slumped awkwardly onto a narrow stone bench while one of the aliens secured his arms to the column.

He was suddenly aware of how filthy and repulsive he must seem, more like a wildman than the neatly dressed colonists of New Bombay with their emphasis on hygiene. He could smell his own sweat, sour from days of not bathing.

Across the way, he saw Lita and Jilan seated at a long wooden table where First-Among-Mothers sat with them. There seemed to be no menace in the alien's actions toward the girls. He tested the bonds; they were flimsy enough that he could burst free if he had to, but he saw only one exit from the cave that would lead up to the surface, the one they'd come down.

Soon other females appeared carrying large pots made from large nutshells like the one Born-Bent had used to mend the DepCom's sitar; they began ladling the contents out into clay bowls to serve the girls. He, apparently, was not going to be given food.

As if she sensed his thought, Lita turned and glanced at him. "Danyo hungers too," she said in very clear Frehti.

First-Among-Mothers leaned forward and gazed at Lita. "No male eats here but the kipiq."

She used a word Ries had never heard before. In spite of his stomach's protests and the presence of danger, he was excited. He felt an adrenaline rush at the unfolding revelation of mystery. While the form of Frehti First-Among-Mothers used ranged from the simpler, chirping utterances of males in the marketplace to more complex constructions, he knew that no lingster encountering it would question the high sentience quotient of the speaker. He had difficulty following it at times, accustomed as he was to the male form of the language.

And he understood now why those first lingsters had been so mistaken in their judgment: They'd forged interface with the wrong sex.

"Danyo is a . . ." Lita struggled but didn't find a word for it in Frehti. ". . . a *lingster*."

Lightheaded from hunger, he almost laughed, remembering an old student joke: *What comes in two sexes but has no sex life? A lingster.*

First-Among-Mothers glanced at him. "The tale arrives before the male. A vragim comes from Sorrow-Crossing and speaks our words."

"I am vragim too," Lita said, jutting her chin stubbornly.

It surprised him to find the girl arguing in his defense. A lot of things about her that he still didn't understand. Her handling of Frehti was one; the DepCom's daughter used the new word as confidently as if she'd always known what it meant.

First-Among-Mothers got up and came over to him.

"Vragim. *Lingster*," she said. If she'd been human he would've read contempt in her tone, but he must resist making connections that might not be there at all. "And do you know how words make, as the tale is told to me?"

He blinked, hearing Born-Bent's voice in memory, *"You understand how words make."* He jumped suddenly between the known and the hidden, the leap of faith every lingster performed at some point, the lucky guess that was also one of humankind's most basic tools for learning language.

"I bring the kipiq's soul home for the Mothers to make words with," he said.

The effect in the stone cavern was electrifying. Every Mother set down her work or her food and stared. Others crowded in from rooms off the main hall till there were at least forty old Freh females gaping at him, round-eyed as owls. A long silence followed, broken only by the clatter of the child's bowl; Jilan seemed the only one in the cavern not affected by his words.

He closed his eyes for a second against his body's weakness, seeking strength to prevail in the battle of wills he sensed had been set in motion.

First-Among-Mothers held out her hand, palm up, and he was startled by her look of almost desperate desire.

"Give."

"No."

She thought about that for a moment, then turned and snapped her fingers. A bent figure hobbled quickly forward and undid the bonds holding his arms. Another followed with a bowl full of the thick stew.

So she thought she was going to bribe him with food?

His stomach insisted it was a fine idea.

First-Among-Mothers waited while he wolfed the contents down without tasting. A second bowl appeared, and he devoured that too, barely noticing how rich and spicy it was this time. When the third bowlful arrived, he was able to eat with a semblance of manners that would've been acceptable in the Guild's refectory.

First-Among-Mothers gestured to the gathered females and they moved silently away. He saw one old alien carrying Jilan, and Lita following them. The main cavern emptied slowly out.

"Now," First-Among-Mothers said. "We make the words together."

*****

He followed her through a low arch at the far end of the big cavern, and came to a smaller cave. The light was dimmer here, and it took a moment for his eyes to adjust. When they did, he saw the Mothers waiting silently in a circle. His breath caught in his chest.

The old aliens had stripped off and discarded their shapeless robes. The flickering light of wax tapers glowed on naked flanks and fleshless rumps, touching with silver the grey fur on their heads, sliding past bony shoulders and spilling over flat, shriveled breasts.

One emaciated female turned her back to him, and he saw clearly knobs of vertebrae and sharp blades of bone outlined under the skin that he identified as ribs, though they didn't appear to be assembled in the human plan. Although Freh females' faces were never tattooed, decoration covered their trunks and all four limbs in scrolls, swirls, leaves and vines. Primitive, by the standards of high civilizations in the Arm, but full of energy and power, the tattoos were dark purple, the color of *zyth* berries.

He'd never seen a roomful of nude women, let alone old women — It was next to impossible not to think of them as women; they seemed more human unclothed as if spirit was more important than species — but he felt no awkwardness. They wore their years with dignity and a kind of patient beauty like a ring of wise elder goddesses.

Now First-Among-Mothers also dropped her garments on the floor, kicking them impatiently against the cave wall. Nakedness seemed to make her grow taller than the others, her body straighter than theirs though no less slack and wrinkled, her grey head fur still partly dark. Like the others, her body was covered in intricate purple designs. The circle opened to let her through.

She walked slowly clockwise inside the ring which began to move counter-clockwise around her. There was something on the ground inside the ring, a center which First-Among-Mothers was circling, an irregularly shaped mosaic formed by small bones, all about the same width and length of the one Born-Bent had entrusted to him. To one side, there were several haphazard, smaller piles. There must've been well over two hundred bones in the pattern, but it looked unfinished, with many spaces and gaps interrupting whatever design was in the process of being formed.

Some kind of religious ceremony, he guessed, watching her circling slowly, her bare feet marking an intricate rhythm on the stone floor. Then she stopped, caught up a bone from the pattern, raised her arms and began to gesture. Her hands caught the tapers' light, sweeping in a broad arc above her head. She seemed to be inscribing some kind of ephemeral calligraphy on the air. As she did so, she opened her mouth and sang one note. Now all the Mothers followed her lead, performing the looping arm movements, the singing tone in unison.

First-Among-Mothers repeated this with each of the bones in turn, marking each with a different sound. Then, after a long while, the group fell silent, the outer circle opened again, and the malformed male Freh who'd stood over Ries on the mountain appeared. The kipiq, who was naked too, entered the circle humbly, shuffling forward over the stone floor on bare knees and holding one hand high above his head. In it, Ries saw a another small bone like the one in his pocket.

Now a low, animal hum broke the silence, rising quickly in pitch and volume. The sound became almost deafening in the confined space, then stopped abruptly as the kipiq reached the center of the ring. He took his time choosing a place to set the bone he carried. In the silence, First-Among-Mothers squatted to see it. The kipiq remained on his knees, head bowed.

She examined the bone, holding it close, turning it, shifting its position, exchanging it with others. At times she seemed to change her mind and returned a bone to its original position, removing another that had now apparently become less desirable and tossing it on the outer piles. Whatever these decisions meant, Ries sensed they were of the utmost importance to the assembled Freh. At last she put a hand on the kipiq's shoulder and the ring of Mothers gave a long drawn-out sigh.

First-Among-Mothers turned, and Ries could see her owl eyes glowing in the light from the nearest taper. She held up the kipiq's bone. Now he saw it had marks scratched on it, like the one in his pocket. Then accompanied by another elaborate hand movement above her head, she sang out a clear, distinct syllable. As she did so, the Mothers followed her arm movements and repeated the sound after her like children performing rote learning. It reminded him suddenly of how, hundreds of years ago on Earth, Chinese children had learned by tracing the characters of their language on the air.

The revelation of what she was doing stunned him. First-Among-Mothers was reading the bones.

But these couldn't be complete words, he realized in a great rush of comprehension, not even morphemes, the smallest units of meaning. The Freh had no written language. She was taking the first step, inventing a system of codifying the phonemes, the individual units of sound. From the gathered bones at her feet, she was choosing the best symbols to begin writing her language.

It was obvious from what he'd observed that not just any shape on a bone would do. Creating a written language was a sacred job, not one to be completed hastily. *Through me flows the meaning of the universe.* He thought First-Among-Mothers would understand the Guild's philosophy very well.

Runes, hieroglyphs, logograms, ideograms, pictograms, alphabets, humans had tried them all through long millennia of experimentation. The Guild taught lingsters in a few years what had taken centuries to unlock, the secrets of these scripts. All but the main one: how they had come into being in the first place. He'd always wondered what accidents of chance and intelligence had caused early humans to take the first step, associating sounds with symbols then developing them into script. And from that to go on to write laws and poems, shopping lists and equations that guided starships across the darkness of space to a world that still stood on the threshold.

The Guild itself with all its research hadn't been able to answer that question, not even for one Terran language. A great wave of exhilaration washed over him. He was witnessing an alien species set out on that mysterious journey. Yet he could also see First-Among-Mothers had a long way to go before the symbols she was collecting were usable.

After a while, she fell silent. The kipiq shuffled back out of the circle into the shadows at the edge of the cave. Ries was aware of her gaze on him now.

It was his turn. The bone containing the symbol Born-Bent found so vital he called it his "soul" must be added to the collection growing at the feet of First-Among-Mothers. The ring of old females gazed at him, waiting patiently. But even in his excited state, a sense of human pride restrained him. He was not going to remove his clothes, nor would he enter the circle on his knees. If the Mothers wanted Born-Bent's soul, they would have to take it his way or not at all.

Conscious of the weight of a shared destiny, human and Freh, he walked solemnly forward in the silence and leaned down, placing the bone in a vacant space.

First-Among-Mothers squatted, peering at the bone as she had done before. Now she reached for it, squinting in the glimmering light. For a long time she studied the symbol scratched there. Then her hand dropped slowly to her side. She stood and faced Ries, her expression bleak.

"Broken," First-Among-Mothers said. "The soul is gone."

Around the ring, old Mothers began to wail.

FIFTEEN

"Think about the waste," Lita said to him. "The tragedy, as the Mothers see it."

The girl had been his only visitor since a group of females had dragged him off to a small niche in a corridor off the main cavern and barred the entrance with a strong lattice of wooden branches lashed with vines. The alcove had probably been a vegetable storage area, he guessed from the lingering smells.

Lita passed a cup of water through the lattice gate and he took a sip. In her other hand she held a slim taper that made deep shadows jump in his cell. He felt exhausted; all emotion and energy had been sucked out of him.

It was hard to estimate the passage of time in this darkness, but he guessed a day had passed since First-Among-Mother's ceremonial reading of the symbols on the bones. While he'd been stuck here, contemplating the consequences of one moment of bad temper, Lita had apparently been deep in conversation with First-Among-Mothers.

Her ability shouldn't have been surprising. She'd been about eight or nine when the family came to Krishna, an age when children still learned languages with some ease, and she must've been exposed to the more complex forms used by the house servants who were largely female. She'd just never let him see evidence of it.

"Freh males don't contribute to the work. Except the kipiq, of course, and not too many of them make it to adulthood."

"I imagine not," he agreed, thinking of the day he and the DepCom had encountered Born-Bent in the bazaar. In his experience of cultures of the Arm including early human, such deformities had usually signaled a short life for the child born with them.

"Do you understand how serious this is, Danyo?" Her face in half-shadow, she looked as if she were thinking about leaving him alone again. "The race doesn't use language like humans. Freh males have a very simple version. Sort of like Kitchen Frehti. Without the Inglis words, of course."

He had the absurd fantasy he was back at the Mother House taking an exam about pidgins and Creoles. "It's uncommon to find such a wide division in ability between the sexes."

"The females are *much* better at it. But the big thing is, up here, year after year for a long time, the Mothers've been working on finding a way to get the language written down."

"You've learned an impressive amount in such a short time."

"Well," she said, softening her tone a little, "I might've missed a few things. I'm not really perfect in Frehti yet. Anyway, every Mother who manages to come up here contributes something. And the one who is 'First-Among-Mothers' puts it all together."

"Why are symbols from the sports so important?"

"The *kipiq*," she corrected, "are male. First-Among-Mothers says the language must balance between male and female or the race will eventually destroy itself. But regular males don't use language well, and kipiqs usually don't survive to be adults, so they don't get very many male symbols. So when the one you brought was broken, they were upset."

It was as if he could hear First-Among-Mother's words echoing through Lita's, and he had the sense that the Freh meant something he couldn't fathom yet.

"The Mothers believe if they can write the language down, they'll have a chance to prevent something bad from happening. Do you understand, Danyo? Can you follow this?"

"Does she say why there are no old males up here, only old females?"

"She said it was the — the — Oh, a word I don't understand. *Sem yaj* — something."

"Sem yaji nuq," First-Among-Mothers said. She had come to stand in the shadows behind Lita.

"Tell me in other words, words I can understand," he said, switching to Frehti.

"Sem yaji nuq. No other words." She turned to Lita and said kindly, "The little one calls you."

Lita went away, taking the taper with her. In the darkness, he was aware of First-Among-Mother's soft breathing.

"No male comes here except the kipiq who brings his soul bone," she said. "Now I must kill you."

He was suddenly exasperated with her mysteries and evasions. "Explain the death of these children's father, and maybe I can help you speed up the work."

"You bargain with me?"

"Yes, I bargain with you."

She hesitated, thinking it over. Then she said, "He learned about sem yaji nuq."

"I do not understand those words. Use others."

"I have not your skill."

"You accepted my bargain."

Her voice rose in anger. "He knew about Those-Who-Have-Gone-Over. You call them *Mules*, but that is your word, not ours."

He peered through darkness, wishing he could see her expression. Lingsters learned to use visual clues as well as aural ones to decipher meanings. *"Something I just learned..."* Patel had said. "What is this connection, so important a man must die for knowing it?"

"You have the answer you sought. Keep your word."

If so, he thought, it was an answer he didn't understand, but he was apparently not going to get any further explanation at the moment.

"I have seen many worlds, First-Among-Mothers, spoken many languages. You are not the first people to wrestle with this problem."

She was silent for so long he began to think she'd gone away. Then she said, "In the market they call you Talker. But you cannot help with this."

"You have nothing to lose by letting me try."

He had the feeling she was reading his face, as if her milky old eyes could see in the dark. Then he heard her sigh.

"We have a saying, 'Bone defeats bone, but stone outlives.' I think perhaps you are stone."

"Let me look at the bones, First-Among-Mothers."

In the darkness, he heard her slice the vines holding the lattice with her knife.

SIXTEEN

He squatted on the stone floor, examining the bone pattern, while First-Among-Mothers held a taper so he could see. The air was thick and fragrant with the incense-smell of tapers, making his eyes heavy. He frowned, concentrating. Somewhere in the main cavern, he heard the sounds of the sitar: Lita picking out tunes to soothe her sister.

He stared at the symbols on the bones. The fine etchings had been colored with a dark, rusty ink that might very well have been blood. He was aware of an almost religious quality to the moment. Spread out before him on the rough stone floor of the cave was the birth of a writing system, a script that could capture a language and its speakers' vision of their world. No modern human had ever witnessed such a moment.

Then he remembered Born-Bent's hand in its bloody bandage and he examined the bones more carefully. They were all a similar length and shape, and all of them had once been fingers, he was sure of it. The symbolism of the Mothers's task began with the medium on which it appeared. He was awed that these aliens — judged simple aborigines by the human colonists — cared so much about a project that many of them couldn't possibly even comprehend. He glanced up at First-Among-Mothers.

"Each Mother gives one," she said. "Except the First. She gives all before her death. One by one."

She held up her hands for his inspection. Freh were four-fingered, three forward and a flexible fourth below the palm. He counted three fingers gone out of eight, two from the left hand and one from the right. An alphabet forged in blood, a ritual as demanding as interface and as dangerous, he thought, given the primitive state of medicine on this world. He wondered if he could've found the courage if it had been his ritual.

"The work has taken many, many years," she told him. "The shapes must be just right to hold the sounds that make up our language. Not every one that is given is accepted. It is the work of the First to choose."

She gestured with the taper, indicating he should continue. After a while, she squatted beside him and gazed at the bones as if she too were seeing them for the first time. Forgotten, the taper dripped wax on the floor.

Some of the symbols he examined were carefully and lovingly inscribed; others resembled the first scratchings of a child. Champollion seeing an Egyptian cartouche for the first time might have felt lightheaded like this, he thought, and Niebuhr copying cuneiform inscriptions may have caught his breath in just the same manner as connections became clear. Ries Danyo, drunkard and failed Guild lingster, was becoming part of the galaxy's history.

Many of the finger bones carried obvious pictograms, tiny exquisite glyphs that were suggestive even at first glance of objects from the world of the writers, though he knew better than to suppose the picture necessarily gave the meaning of the sign any more than it had in Egyptian hieroglyphs. Others bore what were apparently semantic symbols, abstract representations of the sounds of Frehti, and these delicately carved logograms had an austere beauty of their own.

Mixed systems were not unprecedented; Earth had seen several, most notably the Egyptian and Mayan scripts. He wasn't particularly surprised to find one evolving here. But eventually all the languages of Earth had found it more convenient to adopt alphabets. The first problem was not the mix of symbols for sounds and glyphs for whole words, but that there were still far too many choices here at present. Some would need to be eliminated.

First-Among-Mothers touched his shoulder. "I will tell the sound of each one."

Then she began essentially to repeat the ceremony he'd witnessed earlier. One by one she picked up the bones and pronounced the sound that went with it, but where earlier she had sung these phonemes as part of a venerable ceremony with the assembled Mothers, now she was content just to vocalize.

Almost immediately he realized the impossibility of working this way. It was like trying to catch one drop out of a stream of water. He didn't have the stamina to sustain this concentration for very long. He needed to impose some kind of order.

Not for the first time since he'd fled New Bombay he thought with regret of the AI left behind. Sorting and identifying so many alien signs without help was a daunting task. But there'd been translators and interpreters long before there'd been lingsters, before computers too; those early pioneers had worked under primitive conditions.

"I need wet clay. And something to mark with, like a cloth merchant keeping tally."

First-Among-Mothers made no reply to the request, and he wondered if the idea of reducing her exalted goal to humble clay seemed like sacrilege to her. If so, she'd have to get used to it; humanity's profoundest laws had first been scratched in clay. She set the taper on the floor and clapped her hands. A moment later, a figure appeared in the cave's low archway. First-Among-Mothers said something in rapid Frehti and the Mother withdrew. They waited in silence.

After a while, the Mother came back with a lump of clay the size of his fist, clammy from the storage bin. He took it and flattened it out, stretching it into a tablet he could use to make a syllabic grid to plot the signs of written Frehti.

*****

The work progressed slowly over a number of hours; he lost track how many. Twice, First-Among-Mothers sent for more tapers and refreshment. He drank water gratefully, and splashed some on his face to ward off drowsiness, but in spite of his recent hunger he couldn't eat. Gradually, he familiarized himself with the symbols so that similarities and repetitions began to appear, and together they weeded the redundancies out. Over and over again, she patiently repeated the sounds that accompanied glyphs and logograms. It was tedious work.

"It goes too slowly," First-Among-Mothers commented.

She was right. It was an enormous task and would take days at this rate, possibly weeks. The early scholars on Earth had spent years unraveling the secrets of cuneiform or Linear B; if he didn't want to spend that much time here in this cave he needed to find some way to speed things up.

In his fieldpack there was a way.

He touched it now, still safe on his belt; since he'd arrived on Krishna, there'd been no occasion to use it. In it, there were two sequences of drugs that lingsters used in interface. The alpha sequence consisted basically of sophisticated neurotransmitters that increased alertness and enhanced the lingster's ability to work at high speed, especially at such routine tasks as analyzing, cataloging, and memorizing. He'd used them many times on other worlds, always when working with an AI that also monitored the dosage; he knew how effective the alpha sequence could be.

That had all been a long time ago, before he'd begun poisoning himself with *zyth*. No way of telling if there'd be a drug interaction, or how severe. He hadn't had any of the Krishnan liquor for several days; perhaps that would lessen the danger. And if not? *"Another time,"* Magister Kai's voice said in his memory, *"you may not be so lucky."* In all his career, he'd done very little to make the Guild proud of him, and much he was ashamed of. This was a risk he had to take.

"I can make it go faster," he said.

He took out the rack of small plastivials and thought about the pills they contained. First-Among-Mothers gazed steadily at him, her round eyes luminous as a nocturnal animal's in the taper light. She'd asked no questions since he'd begun studying the bones, even when he disturbed the careful way she'd laid them out, accepting that whatever he did it would advance her work. He hoped he could reward her faith.

He shook two small brown ovals onto the palm of his hand, then swallowed them. Within seconds, he felt the sudden jolt of the alpha drugs streaming through his veins. Thoughts sped through his brain too fast for words to catch them; his vision sharpened till microscopic details sprang into vivid display, and he could see individual hairs on First-Among-Mother's head even in this dim light, the wrinkles on her face like the paths of long-dry rivers.

Something else, too, something different this time, something flickering at the back of his mind, disappearing when he turned his attention to it. Then it vanished in a great rush of endorphins that lifted and tossed him like a cork.

The work went faster. Connections seemed suddenly illuminated for his recognition, correspondences jumped out at him, were considered, and First-Among-Mothers indicated her choices which he then recorded. A workable Frehti alphabet began to emerge on the clay tablet.

SEVENTEEN

"One sound is missing."

His nerves jumped at the sound of her voice. Absorbed by the work, he'd lost awareness of his surroundings and again he was confused by the passage of time. Disoriented, he gazed at the last of the tapers burning low, flickering in the draft she caused as she stood up from the work. He squinted through the wavering light at the neat chart he'd inscribed on the clay tablet, sixty-seven symbols that best represented the consonants, vowels, and diphthongs of First-Among-Mother's language, chosen from the drawings on the assembled bones.

"A small sound," she continued dreamily. "Not often used. But the very highest of all. I have waited a long time to find its symbol."

"What sound is that, First-Among-Mothers?"

In answer, she formed a small O with her mouth and allowed breath to come sighing through; he could see her curled tongue almost touching her lips, shaping the sound. What emerged was a diphthong with an initial labial, a singing tone as if it came from a flute. She repeated it for him twice more.

A small scuffling noise behind them drew First-Among-Mother's attention and she fell silent.

"I — I am sorry, First-Among-Mothers," Lita said nervously in Frehti from the shadows in the archway. "My sister wandered off — and I just found her. I will take her away."

"Do so."

For the first time, he wondered what First-Among-Mother's life was like before she came up here to live beneath the Maker's Bones. Had she worked in the bazaar for a cloth-merchant mate, or had she cleaned and cooked in a human residence? Had she borne children, and were any of them male, and if so, did she ever think of what had become of them?

First-Among-Mothers waited until the sounds of the children faded. Then she inclined her head toward the small pile of bones remaining on the stone floor, urging him back to work.

He glanced at them, seeing only duplications of symbols that had already been assigned or obvious clumsily drawn discards. There was no sign left over that could correspond to the new sound she'd just made.

She raised a hand and he was aware of the missing fingers. "A holy sound. Not one Talker hears in the market. It is *Wiu*, The White Bird. You will not find its sign there among the ordinary ones. It is a male sound, and a kipiq should give it shape. Now, Talker-from-Sorrow-Crossing must replace the kipiq's soul that he lost."

The high mood of the alpha sequence deserted him as fast as it had come on. Cataloging the symbols on the bones with her help was one thing; that was no different from the regular duties lingsters often performed for their employers. Deliberately adding a human element to an emerging alien alphabet was another.

It was such a temptingly simple thing she asked of him: One sign, just one, from all the possibilities he'd encountered in human history, or from any of the worlds along the Arm for that matter. But even that little gift would be interference from one culture in another's development, and even minor interference was strictly forbidden. Nothing good ever came from violating this rule, however much the people of the less advanced culture wanted it. Like all lingsters, he'd sworn an oath to respect that prime prohibition.

"I cannot do it," he said. "I am sorry."

"Why can you not?"

"I cannot give you a sign that has its roots on the other side of Sorrow-Crossing. Nothing good would come from such a gift."

"I wish the work completed before my death, Talker," she said, her voice as calm as if she discussed the price of a bolt of silk. "And I do not have much time. You will do it or you will die. I will give you one day's turning to decide."

*****

Two Mothers had appeared as if they'd been waiting for her command, and had taken him back to his alcove prison.

Alone in the darkness once again, exhausted, his thoughts drifted. First-Among-Mothers had posed a dilemma for him. To give her what she wanted he must violate his oath. Never in his life had he knowingly done anything big or small that would alter the natural destiny of any of the alien species he'd come in contact with. But to die for the sake of that oath now meant he must violate the promise he'd made Chandra Patel to protect his family. If he died, the girls had no hope of ever reaching the *Calcutta's* base.

Which was more important, interference in a developing culture — such a tiny touch at that, just the one symbol — or the suffering and perhaps death of the DepCom's children? How would the Guild decide?

"Danyo."

He jumped at the sound of her voice. Without knowing the boundary, he'd drifted from thought to sleep. This time Lita hadn't brought water or a taper.

"Danyo, something's wrong with Jilan. She seems very hot and —"

"As you may have noticed, I'm a prisoner here."

"Devi! Why don't you just open the door and walk out?"

He heard the sound of the lattice gate opening.

"How stupid you are sometimes, Danyo. I could tell as soon as I touched it they hadn't lashed the lattice together again."

If First-Among-Mothers had allowed the opportunity for him to escape, then it was because she knew there was nowhere he could escape to, with or without Lita and her sister. The thought frustrated him; he didn't like being defeated by an old Freh female, even one so obviously intelligent.

"Now will you come and see Jilan?"

He felt Lita's impatient hand on his arm, tugging him through the open gate; he let her guide him through the darkness until light seeped into the corridor from the central cavern.

"I don't know what good I can do. I'm not a medic."

"Keep to the wall just to be safe. No sense letting them see you out here."

"Maybe the food didn't agree with her."

"She's been eating Freh food all her life. That's all the amahs ever made for her after they stopped wet-nursing her. She never touched what Mama and I ate. Do hurry up!"

Jilan was sitting cross-legged on a wide stone bench cushioned in bright silk. Tapers burned in a sconce fixed to the cave wall above her head. In their yellow light, he saw colored clay beads strung on a thong, a crude doll made of wood and covered in fur, toys he'd seen Freh children play with under the stalls in the bazaar. Jilan was making marks with a cut reed on a small lump of clay the size of a cloth merchant's tally. By the uneven flamelight, he could see her pixie face looked flushed. He laid a hand on her cheek and felt how warm it was. Lita bent quickly to wipe saliva from the corner of her sister's mouth.

"I've been giving her water."

"Good."

"What else should we do?"

The child didn't look too sick to him.

Then he became aware Jilan was saying something, very softly, almost under her breath, over and over again. No, not saying, *singing* — But not that exactly either. He felt chilled. Possibility shivered up his spine, moved like the touch of a feather across his nerves. He knelt quickly on the pad beside the child who immediately stopped vocalizing.

"Baby, say it again for me," he said. "Please?"

"What is it?" Lita asked.

Jilan stuck a thumb in the corner of her mouth and stared wide-eyed at him.

"Where's the sitar? Get it for me."

Lita scrambled away and was back a moment later with the instrument. He ran his fingers over the five melody strings, searching for the right notes that described the pitch values of Frehti: G#, A, B flat, B. Jilan seemed to be listening intently. Encouraged, he let his fingers wander among these four tones, the drone strings humming under the impromptu melody.

"What're you doing, Danyo?"

Jilan opened her mouth and sang a note.

Not B flat, he realized, somewhere in between B flat and C, a flattened C. The native nut altered the tones he produced, fitting the sounds of the language better than the original gourd. He quickly adjusted the tuning pegs to reflect the subtly different harmonics of the semitone. Now she gave shape to the sound. His hands shook as he realized what he was hearing, the diphthong First-Among-Mothers had pronounced for him: .

"Danyo?"

"Get First-Among-Mothers and meet me in the cave with the bones."

He hooked the sitar over his shoulder, grabbed up the clay block and the writing utensil in one hand, and tucked the child under the other arm. He felt her cheek burning against his as he ran back to the cave.

New tapers flickered in the small cave, eerily lighting the disturbed pattern he and First-Among-Mothers had left behind. He set Jilan down on the stone floor. Silent again, she gazed up at him, her breathing heavy and quick.

"This won't take long, baby."

"Children invent language," the Guild taught. Why not the alphabet too, or at least a small part of it? The child was as close to a pure source as he was likely to find. Her parents might've come from Earth, but she was born on Not-Here — the planet's alien name was suddenly more appropriate than the one the colonists had given it — and she'd never spoken a word of Inglis. It was a near-perfect compromise. As long as First-Among-Mothers accepted it.

SEVENTEEN

"Have you changed your mind, Talker?"

The clouded eyes gleamed like mother-of-pearl in the taper light when he turned to face her. She stood very erect, almost as tall as Lita.

He chose his words with care. "I offer a compromise, First-Among-Mothers."

"No more bargaining. Only one solution. Make the sign to hold that last, holiest of sounds."

"I cannot give you the sign you desire. It is not my gift to give and would only bring you evil. Instead I offer a child from Sorrow-Crossing but born on Not-Here. A vragim from her mother's womb, but nourished with a Freh mother's milk. Let this child make the sign."

First-Among-Mothers gazed skeptically at him in silence.

"The symbol you want from me," he said gently, "would be male, but it would be alien to your world. What I offer now is better. Trust here."

He waited for several long moments more. She said nothing, but she didn't specifically forbid the attempt either. He took the sitar and plucked the flattened C with the nail of his right forefinger. The child gazed up at him, thumb in mouth. She was drooling again.

"Come on, baby," he coaxed. "Sing for me."

He plucked the note again. She removed the thumb from her mouth and copied the semitone the sitar sang.

He heard the smothered gasp of surprise from First-Among-Mothers, and as the note died away he sounded it again. The child gave voice to the diphthong a second time, and this time her small pure voice was joined by the old woman's larger, mellower one.

He laid his palm flat across the strings cutting off the vibration. The child gazed up at him. He set the sitar down and held out the clay tablet to her.

"Draw the sound, Jilan," he said. "Draw *Wiu* here, in the clay."

She took the tablet and the stylus from him and stared at them for a moment, then began to draw. Apart from the child's labored breathing there was no sound at all in the cave. From time to time she smoothed over what she'd done and began again. Finally, she held the tablet up and tilted her head, examining it. Then she held it out, not to him, but to First-Among-Mothers.

Over the child's head, her sister shot him a startled look.

First-Among-Mothers squatted down and took the tablet reverently as if it were holy, peering at it in the dim light. She took her time.

Then, in a soft voice, she said, "I accept the last sign."

He let the breath he'd been holding come sighing out in a whoosh of relief. Leaning forward, he peered at the symbol the child had drawn. The clay tablet held the crude, stick figure of a bird. He discovered that where a moment before he'd been chilled now he was sweating heavily.

First-Among-Mothers laid the tablet down and took the child's hand in both her own, closing her fingers over it. "But it must be written on bone."

Lita got the significance first. "You can't cut a finger off my sister's hand. I won't let you!"

She threw herself at First-Among-Mothers, almost knocking the Freh and the child over.

First-Among-Mothers didn't appear upset by the outburst; instead, she smiled at Ries over the angry girl's head, her grin a terrifying rictus from that almost lipless mouth. Taking the child's hand had been an act of provocation, showing him who held the power here.

"A child's sign, a male's bone together complete the work." She released the child and stood swiftly. Her hand came up with the three-edged knife glittering in it.

His vision seemed clouded, splitting the light from the knife into a rainbow of fire that stung his eyeballs. The universe was full of wonder and beauty, the Guild taught, but it also held much that was painful and cruel. The first lesson Earth's earliest astronauts had learned hundreds of years ago was that space offered suffering as well as glory. *The faint of heart among you*, the Guild warned its young students, *should stay at home.*

It was a small sacrifice she asked of him, and far better him than the child. Humans had been given an extra finger, as if Nature had long ago foreseen this moment and the need for one of her children to help another. He would think of it as payment for the privilege of witnessing the birth of a written language; no other lingster could say that. His head ached with the burden of such knowledge.

"And in return, will you give us safe passage over the mountains to the starship's base?"

"We will guide you to your people, Talker."

"Take Jilan away now," he said to Lita.

"No, Danyo! We're staying right here with you."

First-Among-Mothers nodded as if their presence too was an acceptable part of the ritual. She held out her hand to him, and hesitantly he put his left hand in it. For the first time in days he thought how good a shot of *zyth* would be to steady his nerves.

She drew him down until both of them were on their knees on the floor in a circle of golden light. With one hand, she positioned his on the stone. The other raised the knife.

At the last moment, he found a center of calm within. He didn't flinch as the knife descended.

EIGHTEEN

The weather was cold and clear as they crossed over the stony summit of the Maker's Bones. It was still two hours before dawn, and alien constellations blazed above them in a forever moonless sky. He stopped to gaze at the brilliant river of light that was the home galaxy, Sorrow-Crossing. Somehow the name seemed to fit better here, in the farthest reach of the Arm, than "Milky Way." Dark sky and high altitude combined to make a magnifying lens of the thin air; he squinted at the enormous treasure of stars spilled across black space, half-convinced he could distinguish the one dim pinpoint of light from all the rest that was Earth's Sol.

Lita touched his arm and he started walking again. First-Among-Mothers had given them food for the journey, and she'd sent along two females who knew the mountain paths as guides. The group moved purposefully, not wasting breath on conversation. From time to time a creature chirruped sleepily from an unseen nest, fooled by their passage into thinking it was morning.

Gradually, the pageantry overhead faded, and a breeze came up followed by the first rays of Not-Here's star. Within the hour, the sun shone fiercely down on them; there was little heat in it yet, but he started to sweat again. The air had the clean, clear smell of sun-warmed stone, and it was mercifully free of spores, but he had difficulty breathing and stumbled often on the uneven ground.

Below them on one side of the ridge, the land swept down a hundred kilometers to the valley of Separation River and the alluvial plain where the human colony had been. The other side fell less steeply to the golden sweep of grassland and the starship base. From up here, the planet appeared suddenly new, as if he'd never seen it before, more exotic than his memory of its strangeness the first day he'd landed. Knowing some of its secrets made it more alien, not less.

He felt lightheaded, an aftereffect of the wound to his left hand that still throbbed, and the fact that he'd had no desire to eat much in the days that followed the reading of the bones. Lita scolded him for his lack of interest in food, but he was relieved to be free of both the promptings of hunger and the need for *zyth*.

First-Among-Mothers had bandaged the wound herself, stopping the blood by packing a native moss into the space left by his severed finger, then wrapping it securely in layers of silk. While he still lay on the bed where Jilan had played, he'd seen the Mothers reverently preparing a small cauldron of boiling water into which they'd added herbs to boil his flesh off the bone so the child's symbol could be inscribed properly on it; his head still rang with the sound of their chanting.

For a moment his mind teetered between past and present, then First-Among-Mother's face rose up before him as she'd stood by his bed. *"I am well pleased with the work,"* she'd said. And he'd argued, *"But mysteries remain. Tell me why language belongs to Freh females but not Freh males." "Have you forgotten what Freh means?"* She held up one of her remaining fingers. He'd never really thought about the literal meaning of a word he'd used so casually for two years. He guessed, *"One? First?"* Then he knew: Those-Who-Come-First.

The memory faded and he staggered against one of the Mothers. She grabbed his arm, steadying him, her old eyes peering into his as if assessing his ability to continue the journey. The two Freh females had caught their long skirts up over bony knees and wore animal skin boots laced above their ankles. The level of their energy surprised him; old as they seemed to be, they'd been taking turns carrying Jilan on their backs over the uneven ground.

But at that moment the child skipped beside them, gathering pebbles and flowers along the way, and chattering in Frehti like any three-year-old who'd been born on this world. Since that first sound uttered over the bones, she hadn't stopped babbling in First-Among-

Mother's language. As if a wall had been breached, he thought, allowing the child to express everything she'd saved up for just this moment. Yet it was just another irony of the human experience on this world that the child had found her native tongue at the very moment when she must leave the company of those who spoke it.

"Are you all right, Danyo?" Lita asked, coming alongside him. "We could rest for a few minutes."

He couldn't rest until he'd fulfilled his promise and brought the DepCom's daughters to the safety of the starship's base.

Lita's cool hand touched his forehead. "You're very hot."

He attempted a joke. "Teething. Like Jilan."

He remembered Lita visiting him soon after his *donation* — a word he could deal with without self-pity. She'd tried to distract him from the pain in his hand with gossip: The Mothers were busy practicing writing out the alphabet under First-Among-Mother's direction; the girl had laughed, describing their first clumsy attempts. She also told him Jilan had cut a late molar and her fever had gone away.

"Let me look at your hand again. Maybe it's infected."

"Antibiotics at the base."

"Danyo," the girl said. "Stop trying to be such a hero all the time."

He stared at her, uncomprehending. She stalked off ahead down the rough path. The ferocious sun dazzled his eyes, and his head throbbed again.

"*What has this to do with Those-Who-Have-Gone-Over?*" he'd asked First-Among-Mothers. "*We are one and the same,*" she'd said, "*only you do not see it yet.*"

He thought about her words now as he stood on the path, one hand pressed to his chest, catching his breath. Metamorphosis was not uncommon among species in the Orion Arm; humans had encountered it more frequently than they'd found sentience on the worlds they'd visited. Even on Earth, caterpillars turned into butterflies and tadpoles became frogs without anyone being too surprised. Why shouldn't a pudgy Freh transform into a gaunt Mule? And if it only happened to one sex, it would still be no stranger than a hundred other quirks and tricks of Mother Nature he'd seen elsewhere. Yet butterflies weren't prone to do violence on caterpillars.

"There is more to it than that," he'd argued, thinking of First-Among-Mother's urgent need to write the language out. *"Some secrets remain hidden until their time comes,"* the old Freh had replied. *"And will you tell me then, First-Among-Mothers?" "If we both live, Talker."*

An hour later — Two hours? Three? He seemed to have lost the ability to keep track of time — the party stopped. They'd reached an overlook, the land falling perhaps two hundred meters straight down a cliff. Spirals of dust rose in the heat, and the view before him shimmered hazily as if it were underwater. A vast plain spread out before them, an enormous valley stretching like a lake of grass to a range of mountains on the misty horizon. Huge flocks of bright-skinned, featherless birds rose and fell over gold-green fields, and the sweet smell of the grasslands drifted up on the warm air.

Sweat started out on his forehead and neck, instantly evaporating, and he sneezed once. He squinted through watering eyes into brightness at the goal they'd struggled to reach for so long, the end of their journey.

"There," one of the Mothers said, pointing.

"The *Star of Calcutta*'s base. I see it!" Lita said.

"We go no further," the second Mother said.

"We can make it from here, can't we, Danyo?"

He nodded and wished he hadn't as the sparkling world spun around him. Drunk without *zyth*, he thought.

One Mother handed Lita the sitar she'd been carrying, the other gave her package of food to the girl.

"You are stone," one of them said to him, touching his head gently.

Stone was a much more humble position to aspire to than rock, he thought.

Then both of them started back up the path. He knew they were anxious to rejoin the frenzy of work going on in the cave, writing out the history of their race in order to preserve its memory. And perhaps put an end to violence in some manner he didn't understand. What excitement there'd be in the Mother House when this story got back to the Guild. He could almost see the Head — whoever it would be now — summoning the teachers and the senior students —

"You really are feverish," Lita said.

"I'll get you there. Don't worry."

She stared at him. "*You'll* get *us* there?"

For the next few minutes she was distracted by the antics of her little sister who scampered back and forth across the path, chasing small flying creatures into the thickets. He was able to direct all of his strength into putting one foot in front of the other instead of having to spend it making conversation. For some reason, going downhill was more difficult and took concentration.

The gleaming white domes and communication towers of the starbase grew steadily bigger as they followed the zigzagging path, but the heat increased, slowing their progress so that the nearer they came to the valley floor the longer it seemed to be taking. It didn't seem to bother the two girls, but he found it harder and harder to lift his feet.

"No use," he said, after a while. "I can't go any further."

"We're almost there." Lita adjusted the sitar over her shoulder. "Look. Only about another hundred meters to the perimeter. I can see the gate and the guard house."

He slumped down by the side of the path. Jilan came skipping back and gazed at him, a spray of crimson wildflowers in her fist. The small blooms were the color of the blood that spurted from his hand when First-Among-Mother's knife descended. He put his bandaged hand up to support his head which seemed to weigh more than he remembered.

The child opened her mouth and sang, *"Wiu,"* a note as pure as a bird's.

"Please, get up," Lita said urgently. "I can't carry you."

"You go. I'll wait here."

"They'll be able to help you down there. You just need some good human pharmaceuticals . . ."

As she stared down at him, the hot breeze rising from below teased the coppery hair and brought its faint scent like woodsmoke to his nose, so that for a moment he had the illusion he was looking at Yv.

So long ago. He'd fallen in love with the way Yv's long hair lifted in the warm wind, the hair with its smoky perfume that bewitched him. He could see her clearly in memory, sitting in the shade of a tree when he'd first seen her, her arm around one of that world's younglings who was teaching her to name the flowers that surrounded them. Though he'd always been sharply aware of his alienness on each world he'd visited, Yv had always seemed at home.

Then he knew one question was answered: Yv would've wanted children. And he would've come to love them, too. It felt good just to sit here and think about his wife.

"There. I can see a guard." Lita stood on tiptoe and waved her arms excitedly. "Oh, he doesn't see us. But I'll go get him, and then somebody'll come back for you."

Jilan put her bouquet of wildflowers in his lap and their perfume was so rich it made his head spin. She danced away from him into the light, her slight figure shattering in a myriad diamond points that hurt his eyes to watch. She seemed more an elemental spirit of this world than a human child, and he recognized in that one scintillating moment that there were mysteries that were not given to him to understand.

"You'll be all right?" Lita asked. "It won't take very long."

"Yes. Go."

She hesitated for a moment longer, then leaned down and kissed him quickly on the cheek. "When we get back to Earth, Ries," she said, "I'm going to become a lingster, like you."

He put his hand up to touch his cheek and found it wet with his own tears.

The DepCom's daughters ran down the path to the base, the DepCom's sitar bouncing on the older daughter's back. The running figures became smaller and smaller. Then a tall figure emerged from the gatehouse and hurried toward them. Ries watched till the radiance forced his eyes closed.

When he opened them again, his wife was standing in the wildflowers at the edge of the path, hair spilling like flame over her shoulders. She was wearing the sky-blue wedding dress.

Yv held out her arms to him, welcoming him home.

interlude

INTERLUDE

Stormsinger, First-Among-Mothers, held up her hands, two-fingered, three-fingered, witness of what had been given to the work. Whitebird, beside her on the stone bench, folded her own hands and watched firelight flicker on Stormsinger's skin. Day of threat and promise, begun under New-Eye's rising with Whitebird's secret blood first flowing, ending at nightfall in Stormsinger's hands. Whitebird knew the twin birds of hope and fear.

The hall deep under the Maker's Bones grew dark, but no one stirred to light the lamps. Gabble of shrill voices sank away. All turned eyes to Stormsinger.

"Now," Stormsinger, First-Among-Mothers, said. "Trust here."

Stormsinger looked down the long table at each Mother in turn, and Whitebird looked with her. Some were bent and some were blind, but none dared challenge Stormsinger.

"I choose my successor as every First chose hers."

Stormsinger waited. Cold moved through the hall and silence. The two-fingered hand came to rest on Whitebird's arm.

"I name Whitebird First in turn upon my death."

The hall filled with the sudden hiss of protest.

Longwalker-daughter-of-Birdcatcher-sister-of-two-younger stood to challenge, anger straightening her twisted spine. "Halfgrowns do not lead Folk!"

"Time for new thinking," Stormsinger said.

"She did not give bone." Longwalker held up her own three-fingered hand in witness of her words.

Down the long table Mother leaned to Mother sighing. Hands

fluttered, four-fingered, scarred three-fingered. Breath caught in Whitebird's throat, her own fingers clenched. There was more, but even Longwalker dared not say it in Stormsinger's presence though she did not hold back when she found Whitebird alone.

"We need no bone now," Stormsinger said. "It is done! The time comes when we will need what Whitebird brings."

The spark Stormsinger lit long ago in Whitebird's heart flamed at this prophecy. Halfgrown, newly marked by blood she would not speak of now or ever, she must answer Longwalker's challenge and claim her destiny.

Rising, left hand on the table, right hand on the three-edged knife in her belt, Whitebird held Longwalker's angry gaze. The hall fell silent. Yellow eyes glittered in the flame-lit hall, watching, testing.

Whitebird raised the knife. "I am Folk. I am not afraid to give bone."

The blade sparked red in firelight. She slashed down at the five-fingered hand on the table. A spurt of blood and searing pain — The smallest finger fell away.

The Mothers wailed, their voices echoing. Whitebird's eyes closed in darkness. Stormsinger caught her as she fell.

PART TWO

BRIGHT
RIVER OF TALK

ONE

The last line was a lie, but they expected it, so Lita read it:

"And after that, they all lived long and happily on the colony world."

The scent of new-mown hay drifted through the library's open windows. She closed the paper pages of the old book and glanced at the ring of young children sprawled on the rug. Most of them looked bored. A four-year-old girl, brown curls tied with trembling yellow butterflies, smiled. Tomorrow the child's ornament would be dead.

"Well," she prompted. "Did you like the story?"

"No," a boy said.

He'd told her today was his fifth birthday but she'd have guessed ten from his size. Kids were bigger these days, maybe they were also wiser, able to see through false endings.

She smiled at him. "Why's that?"

"I like it better when the Artis read. Artis can make sims. You can't."

He waved his arms around, punching the air with his fists and making whooshing noises, miming battles between alien hordes and brave human colonists on their way to happy last lines. The librarian, a middle-aged man in a black bodysuit with dazzling laser pinstripes, put a finger to his lips in reproof.

"I like to see them fight," the boy said. "Pow! Bam! Pow!"

The little girl with the butterflies leaned over and punched his shoulder. The librarian separated them.

Lita had spent two hours this morning reading to the group in the library. The AIs these children had at home did the main job of teaching literacy, but old wisdom held human contact was vital in the early years. The Guild of Xenolinguists encouraged its students to volunteer, and although there were other things she'd have much preferred spending her time on, she needed to score points. The Guild insisted on using real books, too, and the opportunity to handle such priceless things was an incentive. Judging from the bored faces surrounding her, either the program wasn't a success or she was a failure.

"Don't take it personally," the librarian murmured as she prepared her retreat to the Mother House.

The boys in the group, released from their obligation to listen politely, tumbled and mock-wrestled on the rug. The girls whispered secrets to each other. No one seemed sorry to see her leave except the librarian.

"I don't have much experience with children," she said.

"No siblings?"

His question provoked a flash of memory — A child with red hair, legs laced in animal-skin boots, spilling alien flowers as she skipped along an alien path. The dull ache of this memory never went away, private pain, not something to share with strangers. "No."

"I'm sorry to hear that."

Families were important, his expression said. Lots of children to colonize lots of worlds. Until the aliens arrived. Pow. Bam. Pow.

"Are you coming back next week?"

The librarian's thin face was lit with eagerness that intensified age lines he either couldn't afford to remove or was proud of as a badge of his neo-retro status. He reminded her of colonists in New Bombay, gaudily attired but too far from Earth to benefit from luxuries such as rejuve. He was old enough to be her father, who might've come to look like the librarian if he'd lived. Maybe he was just excited by the presence of a real book, she thought; librarians in small towns probably didn't see many of those. She walked past him out the main door of the library.

She was a stranger, born on Earth but not at home here anymore. In a few months when she graduated she could go anywhere in the

Orion Arm, anywhere the Guild sent her, and it wouldn't matter to her. Anywhere, except the nightmare world she'd come from. She wondered if it would make any difference, or if she'd feel homeless wherever she went.

The Alps loomed over the library's steep roof, a row of old grandmothers shawled in white keeping an eye on the unruly children. She liked mountains; maybe it was a distant memory of childhood summers at the foot of the Himalayas. Some mountains, she amended the thought; the jagged skeletons called the Maker's Bones weren't on that list.

The road back to the Guild's Mother House in Geneva followed the shining ribbon of the Rhone. The sky grew increasingly overcast, threatening rain.

The noon robobus rolled away down the road just as she arrived at the terminal. There wouldn't be another one for two hours. Settling the priceless book deeper in her pocket, she set out to walk back.

 TWO

Whitebird, First-Among-Mothers dreamed:

A farmer's cart, bright as water, flying.

She lay on her bed, sweat soaking the cushions in the half-darkness of two remaining candles, and willed the wild beating of her heart to slow. Her fingers probed the grey stubble of hair, feeling the ache in knuckles that every day grew stiffer.

Eye-on-Third-Bone-Fifth-Day.

Work to do this day, every day, come sun, come rain, and others would be early about.

In her bedchamber the air was heavy with candle smoke and crushed herbs. Above, the Maker's Bones, the oppressive weight of mountains. Sleep, when it came at all, no longer refreshed as it had when she was younger, believing time endless. Now, like Stormsinger's, her life might end before the work. The work remained. Always the work.

She was shamed by this tiredness in her bones. The work was sacred.

"You are awake, First?" a timid voice asked.

A small female, still chubby with juvenile rolls of fat under a brown robe, stood in the entrance. Candle flame cast bars of light and shadow on a face halfway in color between river clay and dark earth. First read nervousness in raised fur on the young one's head.

"I am awake, Youngest."

She was fond of this little female who brought merry ways and the scent of flowers into a dark place of creaking bones and sour faces. All except First and Youngest had borne young of their own before journeying up the mountain. Her own womb was shriveled and as barren as the third *zyth* berry, perhaps as poisonous. Youngest was a sign of change, and only time would say whether good or bad.

The raised fur went down. Youngest held out a gourd. "I brought this."

Water glittered in candlelight. First was not thirsty, but she took the gourd for the young one's sake and touched it to her lips. Turning in the underground halls and narrow corridors, she often caught Youngest's gaze as if the little Mother wished to speak but was too shy. She was reminded of her own youngling days here, the cosseting and the loneliness of the company of the very old.

"Tell what wakes you," she said.

Youngest was a head shorter than First, with a lipless mouth. As a youngling, First had despaired over her own plump mouth. Odd, she mused, that age had given her the thin lips she had once so desired. And like all the Mothers who came here since Stormsinger's day, Youngest was still four-fingered on both hands.

"I could not sleep, First."

"Tell what troubles you."

Youngest knelt beside First and laid her head on the older female's lap. First stroked Youngest's head fur. The eyes of the Folk were yellow until they whitened with age; her own were dark as tree bark. There had been nothing she could do about her eyes, or the cycle of blood that once marked another difference. But she had taken knife to her hair till it was short and rough like fur.

"I fear you are in danger, Mother."

First knew she had enemies under these mountains. The youngling heard gossip that hushed at her own approach. Softly, softly, she thought. More was soothed with silk than stone. "Tell how the younglings learn."

Youngest spoke eagerly. "They learn faster than grown ones!"

First was happy to hear this. Telling the signs that made words was great work, for the Song of the Folk's beginnings must be learned again. Without it, the Folk died in despair; every season brought fewer and fewer births. The Song would heal, restoring spirit that was lost. The Mothers had written on their own bones for generations to bring this forth.

"I will go with you next time. I will see the younglings learn."

Youngest clasped her hands in front of her face in the sign of joy.

First's own work went further. Those-Who-Have-Gone-Over, brothers lost in madness and rage, must be brought back now. Only then could the Folk be one again. Death might stalk her like a cloudbeast, but she was cunning and would hide from it till her work was done.

"Go now, prepare my morning meal," she said.

Youngest went away.

The dream still bothered. First pressed a hand to her fluttering heart, the eyes of her mind seeing beyond the sleeping chamber. Who might fly in a cart such as she had dreamed? Stormsinger had told of Humans who lived the other side of Sorrow-Crossing. They had come to Not-Here to build dens, but the Folk had driven them away in the days of Great-Fire-Burning-All. First did not like to think about Humans for she knew she was one.

A candle burned out, its smoky scent a luminous haze on the chamber's shadows. Her legs were as heavy as stone this morning, and her heart struggled in her chest like a bird in a trap.

A farmer's cart that flew. Could such a thing be? She looked down at her hands, one four-fingered belonged to the Folk, one five-fingered did not. Stormsinger had said her kin were Human. Did her kin fly like birds in these carts?

Before her death, Stormsinger whispered strange things First had never forgotten. The river of light the Folk called Sorrow-Crossing, a path of exile! A home lost among the bright sky pebbles! *"This we share,"* Stormsinger's voice said in her memory, *"for you too have lost a home the other side of light."*

First craved answers as a youngling craved the teat, but none came. She stared at the last candle; the flame would soon go out. All life followed that pattern, plant or flame or Folk, burning brightly for a time, then vanishing from the world.

Memory swept into her mind: A chamber, vivid in color and pattern. A young female, hair red as *zyth* berries as her own had once been. She remembered a hand stroking, a voice singing — Once she had had a sister-in-blood, Human. The sister-in-blood-one-older had gone away in a flying cart far down the river of light. Long dead by now, for the sister-in-blood was much older.

Humans and Folk, she thought, strung like beads along Sorrow-Crossing. Their beauty tore her heart.

Yet the work waited. Stormsinger had given that too. It was almost done, the words ready now. Soon she must carry them down from the Maker's Bones to those who were lost. A dangerous journey that would be, but it was hers to make, her task while there were still days left to her.

Only the weak feared danger.

Only fools fretted what they could not change.

THREE

Eruditus Ursin Colm, a small old man in a voluminous brown djellaba, acknowledged her with a brief wave when Lita entered his chambers, then turned his attention back to a small screen. With his thin white hair and wispy beard, he seemed like an ancient Indian guru dispensing visions of nirvana from a mountaintop, the kind of ethereal wisdom her mother had been fond of quoting but not following. She saw it reflected in the phrase from the lingster's mantra he'd carved over the stone fireplace: *First was the Word.*

Colm was the only member of the senior faculty who'd taken an interest in her. Fifteen when she'd arrived five years ago, she'd been old by Guild standards; the Guild liked to start training lingsters at the age of five. Colm offered tutoring in exchange for performing household tasks he was no longer up to doing for himself. His chambers were sparsely furnished, his needs few, the work wasn't onerous.

Today, the eruditus had a guest, a Venatixi, the first time Lita had seen one outside of vids her father had showed her. Her palms were instantly clammy; these aliens were the reason for the starship base on Not-Here, maintained long after the sudden end of the Human-Venatixi war.

The alien wore a white toga, but if there were overt sexual characteristics to the Venatixi, she didn't recognize them. Yet the impression the alien made was overwhelmingly male. In vivid contrast to his host, he was three meters tall with milky gold skin and darker gold hair. She found it hard not to stare at him; his was a beauty that suggested a sculptor's glorious ideal rather than the more shopworn reality of humans.

"Jas'Alak," Colm said, "I present my student, Lita Patel."

The alien's name involved a difficult glottal stop, common in the Venatixi language from what little she knew of it.

She used an honorific: "Mer."

The Venatixi's eyes picked up light from the study's tall windows. She'd seen eyes that glowing amber color once before in an old alien called First-Among-Mothers. The Freh's eyes had flashed with humor or cunning as the mood took her, but the Venatixi's were as empty as stone. She understood now the horror reported by veterans: Humans had fought angels and lost. She was disturbed to learn Colm had one as a friend. Yet these enigmatic beings had shown no interest in pursuing victory; they had simply withdrawn, leaving humans still uncertain what the war had been about.

Ursin Colm and his visitor continued their conversation in Venatixi. Lita took a hot-stone out of its box on a shelf to make tea for them. Through the open window came the sound of young voices, Guild students off to spend a lazy afternoon sailing, soaking up the last of summer's warmth. She'd never found the time to go to the lake, and no one had tried to persuade her.

The water in the kettle boiled in ten seconds. She added a pinch of tea, then set two of Colm's favorite porcelain cups on a tray and took them to him.

The Venatixi had gone.

Colm picked up one cup and sipped the hot tea as if the alien had never been there at all.

"I thought — I mean, I made two cups —"

"Sit, drink one," Colm said affably. "It's just their way. Would you like to see the progress I've made?"

Since he obviously wasn't going to explain his vanished guest, it would be rude for her not to do so. She nodded, relieved to have the uncomfortable presence of the alien removed.

He lifted his hand and the air shimmered. Columns of Inglis words glittered like fireflies. She recognized the abbreviated list of words showing the greatest tendency toward stability in the long evolution of

Earth's languages:

I/Me. Two/You. Blood. Water. Finger/One. Hand. Sun. Night.

The original list, developed centuries ago by early linguists such as Pinker and Ruhlen, had established the single-origin theory of all human languages. Colm selected from that list those essential words more likely to appear in alien languages. Not every species had noticeable ears, could weep tears, or had tasted salt, so those words were left off his list, but all orbited their star and knew the absence of light called night in Inglis.

The AI Colm employed was far more powerful than a household Arti making sims for the children. Lita suspected now it might be manufactured by the Venatixi; lingsters who encountered Venatixi AIs in the field were impressed but wary of them. Colm seemed undisturbed. The sparkling columns began to scroll. Linguistic history flowed backward from the forms the core words assumed in present-day Inglis through earlier incarnations in the many language families that had once existed, back through vast stretches of time to their reconstructed proto-versions.

"Now watch," Colm said.

Faintly at first, then growing brighter, other lists came to shadow the Inglis words, alien words from languages Guild lingsters had collected up and down the Orion Arm.

She leaned forward to read. The flow stopped at the point where her eyes focused, resuming when she looked away. Alien words sharpened into legibility, equivalencies for the Inglis words they clustered with. A few were familiar, words from Omareemeean, Gai'eki, Tlokee, the High Tongue of Ozal, RsS'n A and RsS'n B. Not every human word had an alien counterpart; some areas were thickly populated, others sparse from lack of data.

Then words in Frehti leaped out, and a spasm of fear followed by a disorienting homesickness caught her. She couldn't forget the fires or the smell of blood. She would remember Krishna as long as she lived.

The eruditus pulled his chair closer, leaning into the shimmering symbols and frowning in concentration.

"See here? The connection 'one' with 'finger' clearly occurs in Venatician and Almeranti, just as it does in many of our own early languages. The fact that we and the Venatixi are five-fingered but Almerans are four-fingered and four-toed makes no difference."

The Freh were four-fingered, until the Mothers each sacrificed a digit for the sake of their language. She turned her head away so the old man wouldn't notice her eyes filling with tears.

Colm noticed. "I fear I've disturbed unhappy memories."

She shook her head. She'd survived; others hadn't. She hadn't deserved her luck, but it was her curse to carry alone. "It's nothing. I'll tidy your room now."

"No," he said, snapping his fingers to dismiss the screen. "We'll take a break, my dear. A walk in the orchards will breathe new life into both of us."

FOUR

Candlelight dappled the hall under the Maker's Bones in amber. The high ceiling where shadows caught was strung with drying vegetables; their sharp perfumes mingled with the smoky odor of burning wax. Over it all lay the bitter scent of *zyth* berries boiling in a cauldron at the back of the cooking fire. First-Among-Mothers leaned on the table and caught her breath.

The work going forward in this place had swallowed the lightness of her youngling days, chewed up the love she had found, and now gaped ready to devour her success at the last. Her whole life had been hostage to the work, Stormsinger had seen to that. Yet while she still had breath she would not weaken. She stood tall, back stiff, eyes narrowed against any that might challenge, even Death itself, and looked down the long table.

Two younger Mothers spread narrow sheets of grey tree skin over the wood. The skin had been soaked in tubs, then flattened and pounded and spread to dry. In Stormsinger's day, the signs that carried sound had been scratched into clay. But that was slow and tedious, and clay tablets heavy for old Mothers to carry.

Mothers came to sit on either side down the table's length; one sharpened sticks for making the signs. First sat on a bench at one end and studied them.

Four at table were slow-thinking, unable to hold any thought long, and five more never spoke at all; First ignored them. Darkleaf-sister-of-one-older, and sister-in-heart to Whitebird, sat near the fire. Small, her face crumpled like the winter leaves she was named for, bent almost in half by the treachery of time, Darkleaf's beauty lay in the kindness of her hands, ever ready to comfort and help. First would have liked to touch them now, but the time for such comfort had slipped away. Darkleaf too must be left behind, and all that endured was the work.

The last Mother at table was Rockgiver-sister-of-two-older, skin transparent as ice, the greenish light of bones showing through. First gazed long at this one. Rockgiver, younger sister of Longwalker, last Mother to give bone to the work, neither forgot nor forgave. Hers was the voice whispering disapproval and reproach that Youngest heard.

Youngest took her place at the other end of the table, facing First. The young female had brought with her rolls of the prepared tree skin, and these she passed to the Mothers. First had worked out the better way, and she had named it "Skin-carrying-the-message-of-bone," for the signs had first been made on bone. The Mothers shortened this to "skinbone," and then to "skin."

"We are ready. Tell the words of the Song," First said.

Youngest took another skin from a pocket in her robe and unrolled it, smoothing it on the table. She began to tell aloud the words, a few at a time so even the slowest of Mothers could copy them down on the blank rolls. The Song had been gathered from many, many Folk who each knew a little part till it was whole again.

Words themselves held all the mysteries of life, First thought. Nothing could be without words to name it. Perhaps words had even spun the Eye awake in the beginning, their power was so great. If there had been no words, would there have been no worlds and no Folk? Did words in fact create everything that was?

Where did these thoughts come from that tormented her?

Pressing one hand to her chest where dull pain lurked, she focused on Youngest's voice rising over the scratch of sticks and the hiss and pop of candle flame in the drafty hall.

Youngest told the story of Freh beginnings:

The Song of The Folk

The scar appeared on the Eye at the time of Rain-Catcher's birthing.

"Does the Eye fight?" Rain-Catcher asked her first mate.

"How could that be?" Den-Builder said.

Rain-Catcher and her first mate curled together in the ternary's den under Middle Hill, arm to arm and leg to leg.

"The youngling within slows your thought." He patted her swollen belly. "Mine," he added.

The Eye flooded the rocky plains with dazzling light, and Here wavered in the heat. A dark smear showed on its upper half. Rain-Catcher felt the stab of fear. Her tongue flickered, tasting her first mate. The youngling kicked against her belly, anxious to be born.

A shadow filled the den's entrance. Night-Singer, second mate, third of their ternary, was growing taller than both, and although he had only just Gone Over, his skin had whitened and now folded over his bones.

Night-Singer said, "I have been far beyond these hills. I have seen strange ones. Not-Folk."

Den-Builder said, "Not-Folk cannot be. You are shadow dreaming."

Rain-Catcher knew her first mate had secretly hoped the change would come to his body, not Night-Singer's. The Eye caused only one male in a ternary to change, and she knew in her heart it was Night-Singer who planted the seed, for she had mated with Den-Builder many times and no youngling started, with Night-Singer only once.

Night-Singer began to sing:

"I have seen ugly ones
They are covered in hair
The color of sand
Their eyes are straight
Not round like the Eye
Or the eyes of the Folk."

The Three Hills Folk never scratched at wounds for long. Soon the youngling determined to be born, and all three attended to its arrival. Rain-Catcher pushed, and Den-Builder patted, and Night-Singer sang. It came squalling out into Den-Builder's waiting hands. Den-Builder bit the cord and licked it clean.

Then the three of them carried the youngling outside the den. They stood at the foot of Middle Hill, offering its body to the night sky so it might gain spirit. Though the Eye that watched by day was fierce, the night sky was thick with pebbles of fire and only a little less bright.

One day, Den-Builder squinted at the Eye.

"The wound grows," he told her. "It is bigger now."

A strange noise boomed in the distance beyond Small Hill where mountains loomed in haze. Other ternaries came out of their dens.

Rain-Catcher looked. The Eye bore a bruise over most of the upper half and spreading below.

"We must seek Those-Who-Have-Gone-Over," Den-Builder said.

The Folk made their way up Tall Hill where the wise ones gathered. Rain's footsteps boomed in the air, but no rain came, and sometimes they were so loud she felt them in the land under her feet. The wise ones sat in a circle at the top.

Den-Builder pointed at the Eye. "What does it mean?"

Those-Who-Have-Gone-Over looked at each other without speaking.

At last, Oldest lifted up his long head. "We must build a tower of stone to honor the Eye."

The Folk stretched out empty hands, fingers splayed, holding no meaning. Those-Who-Have-Gone-Over kept the wisdom of the Folk, and Oldest was wisest of them all.

Then Rain-Catcher saw a strange sight. Two huge black beasts, twice as tall as the tallest of Those-Who-Have-Gone-Over, climbed up the steep path. They moved on four legs that seemed too thin for the muscular bodies perched on top, and some of the joints folded backward. Two long arms with cunning fingers reached and plucked as they walked. Heads stuck out from their bodies on slender necks. The eyes of these beasts were slits. Her second mate came up the path behind the beasts.

One of the beasts opened its mouth and made noise. The sound was so terrible that the Folk covered their ears.

Night-Singer stepped forward and sang:

"From the sky
They come
Work to do
Listen
They try to speak."

Night-Singer held his hands out, eight fingers splayed, empty of answers.

The second beast stepped forward. Now Rain-Catcher saw it carried something small the color of wet stone, yet shaped like a basket with a lid. She had no word for the thing. The beast placed the odd thing on the ground and touched it.

A shrill voice came out. "Greetings — No harm —"

Night-Singer said, "For three days I sang to this basket thing. Now it speaks for the Not-Folk. I hold no meaning for this."

"You will go to a new home." The thing's voice was now smooth as water.

Oldest stood up slowly, letting folds of loose skin settle over his long bones. "Where would the Folk go? Our dens are Here."

The thing said, "A better land for dens. A land where water runs in all seasons and plants grow taller than folk."

Then all the Folk held their hands out, fingers splayed, at such shadow dreaming.

"Here will not exist much longer," the thing said. "If you stay, you will die."

"Who are you?" Den-Builder demanded.

"We build —"

Both beasts stood stiffly on four legs and gestured with two long-fingered hands, cupping them together as if they cradled younglings. They stopped and pointed at the Eye.

"Circles. Rings." The beasts pointed again at the Eye. "There will be nothing left of Here. Hurry, or it will be too late for you."

"They speak of other lands in the sky, and other Eyes to bless them." Night-Singer held out empty hands. "No meaning."

The beasts picked up the talking thing and started back down the path. Then they stopped and looked back.

"You are the last," the thing said.

*****

Pain stabbed, snatching the breath out of First's mouth and bringing darkness to her eyes, banishing the sound of Youngest's voice telling the words of the Song. She clutched at the table.

Darkleaf-sister-in-heart was instantly at her side. After a moment, sight returned and she saw Youngest's stricken face, fur standing straight up on her head.

"I will stand alone," she said when breath returned, brushing off Darkleaf's support, unwilling to show weakness in Rockgiver's presence. "I am . . . only a little tired."

The telling and copying would go on without her. But she knew, she knew. She too was the last, and if her time ran out before she had done what must be done, all would be lost. Darkleaf hovered beside her as she walked, arms ready to catch if she stumbled. She reached the chamber without the need for aid.

The candles had all burned out. Darkness was a presence in her chamber, Death the Assassin, waiting to swallow her breath.

"Soon you may have me, but not yet," she said aloud.

Puzzled, Darkleaf turned to gaze at her, hands outstretched to caress.

First pushed her away.

 # FIVE

They sat on a stone bench in the shade of apple trees planted when the Guild was young. Ancient and gnarled now, the trees were cherished as old friends from whom nothing was expected. Here and there in the half-dead branches, a few spots glowed orange-gold with the last fruit, not enough to harvest and all too often wormy inside.

"Trees are our relatives," Colm said, gazing up through a lacework of black twigs. "Who knows what slow thoughts a tree has? Vast and ponderous chemical messages in the sap. We can't read them yet. Someday, perhaps."

She glanced at him, expecting to find him smiling, teasing her into a lighter mood, but his expression was serious. Ursin Colm, his name meant both bear and dove. Mostly dove, she decided.

"Life is everywhere rich in contradiction and complexity, you see, but nothing is impossible for science to unravel given time." He laid a wrinkled hand on her smooth brown one. "Now tell me what this sorrow is that you carry today."

"When I came here, Eruditus, I dreamed of keeping a promise and becoming a lingster. I won't be allowed to keep it."

She'd come from a life of family and privilege to find herself orphaned, an outsider who made no friends, a colony brat with no hope of being fully accepted in Earth society no matter how hard she studied. A survivor dragging a trunkful of guilt and no way to put it down.

"You're a good student. Learning Frehti as a child helped. But you see, the Guild likes to start training a lingster very early."

"So I'll be a translator. I'll translate shopping lists if that's all Magistra allows."

Memory unfolded: The native market outside New Bombay's wall, Ries Danyo translating the price of cloth for her mother — She swallowed hard.

"Tell me your story," he said.

*****

"When we get back to Earth," she'd promised, "I'm going to become a lingster, like you."

Ries Danyo's cheek had been wet with tears, and even then she knew the lingster wasn't going to live long enough for her to fetch help. She couldn't stay here with him on this hillside. She had to get her sister to the *Star of Calcutta*'s base.

Taking Jilan's hand, she ran down through brilliant flowers toward the buildings and the sentry who'd just spotted them, her father's sitar bumping and jostling on her back. Three-year-old Jilan got there first, and the tall man swept her up in his arms.

"You're the DepCom's kids! What're you doing here?"

"We need help," she said.

"We thought you'd all been killed!"

In the crew mess, the sentry handed them over to another man who identified himself as Lieutenant Shastri. He had the gangly, unhinged walk that marked those who spent much of their lives on low-gravity ships.

They sat on benches either side of a plain table in a room so stark it made her shudder. Her mother had ornamented and embellished the Residence in New Bombay until it was like living inside a jewel box. All that beauty gone now, lost in the fire.

"We left a man up there on the hill," she said. "A lingster. I think he's dead."

Shastri poured chai into plain cups, his dark eyes watchful. "With the *Calcutta* gone, there's only a skeleton crew, three of us."

"Danyo saved our lives."

Shastri nodded. "We'll bring the body in later."

He set bowls of kedgeree before them and plates of naan. Jilan ate ravenously.

"When do you expect the ship back?"

"Tomorrow. We sent word as soon as we heard about New Bombay. There was never a hint something like that could happen."

"It's monsoon. The season for the Mules to cause trouble!"

Shastri said carefully, "Somebody made a bad decision."

"And as a result my parents are both dead. Now it's your responsibility to get us back to Earth to my father's people."

"There's been fighting around here too," the lieutenant observed.

She stared at him until he colored and turned away. She finished her meal in a silence broken only by her sister's singsong that she recognized suddenly as the Frehti alphabet the Mothers had recited in the cave under the Maker's Bones where they'd found temporary shelter. One sound stood out above the rest, the one Jilan had contributed: *Wiu.*

Shastri stood up. "You'll want to change clothes. We can probably find something to fit you from one of the female crew's wardrobe. Don't know about the little girl, though."

"Improvise." She saw how he bit his lip, holding in the reply he'd have liked to make. "My sister needs to sleep. We'll require two bunks."

"Follow me," he said tightly.

During the night, Danyo's body was brought in. She heard men's muted voices as they passed her door. She slept fitfully. The old alien called First-Among-Mothers stalked her dreams, blood-stained knife in her hand.

Next morning, Shastri woke her just before dawn to tell her of a change in plan.

"It's too dangerous to have the *Calcutta* land. Mules've been sighted in the area."

"A starship has to fear a band of savages?"

"They're sending down a shuttle to pick you up."

Lita dressed Jilan in the oversized grey sweater and long socks

Shastri had found for her, lacing over them the animal skin boots First-Among-Mothers had given the child before they left.

"We're going home to Earth," she told Jilan.

She'd hated coming to Krishna with her parents, leaving schoolfriends, her pet monkey, the peacocks strutting through the gardens of the Patels' summer house in India. Now she was going back and leaving her parents here — dead, unburied.

The little girl turned large, dark eyes toward Lita, and she felt suddenly as if she didn't know her sister at all. The moment passed and they went outside.

They emerged into a cold, ashen light on the landing pad, and a stiff breeze whipping the flag of the United Earth. The Milky Way galaxy the Freh called "Sorrow-Crossing" still showed faintly overhead between tattered night clouds. Beyond the perimeter of the base lay the vast, level prairies of the continent's interior stretching mistily to the horizon. Shastri and the third member of the skeleton crew stood together, rubbing their arms and talking in low tones.

Movement in the shadow of a wall drew her attention. A stooped Freh female in a shapeless dun garment watched them, her subservient manner like all the docile Freh Lita had ever known until she'd met First-Among-Mothers. She grasped Jilan's hand tightly and turned her eyes to the grey sky, scanning for the approach of the shuttle. A flock of small, featherless birds swooped overhead. Now the first rays of the rising sun gilded the tops of antennae on the roof of the *Calcutta*'s base.

Then the shuttle loomed, positioning itself over the center of the painted bullseye. She felt its downdraught and clutched the borrowed crew jacket closer. The small craft settled to the ground with a sigh. The door opened. A blonde female crewmember gazed down at them.

"Right," Lieutenant Shastri said, and she heard relief in his voice. "On board with you!"

The woman held out her hand to help them up the ramp.

A horde of naked male Freh came running around the corner of the building, screaming and brandishing knives. Hideous purple tattoos covered their faces like war paint. In their midst, towering above them, his skin hanging on his bones like clothes on a hanger, she saw a Mule.

All the horror of the past two weeks came raging back. The revolt of the normally placid Freh houseboys — the murder of her parents at the Residence in New Bombay — her first, sickening sight in the jungle of the second race on Krishna —

The lieutenant went down in a spurt of blood. The other man fought for a moment, then he too dropped. The air was filled with the ear-shattering ululation of Freh voices.

"Get on board!" The blonde woman held out her hand. "Now!"

Lita stumbled up the steps, panting with fear, dragging Jilan as the Freh surged toward the shuttle. She reached for the woman's hand.

At the last moment Jilan tugged free and turned back.

"Amah!" the child cried.

Jilan ran straight into the oncoming aliens. Lita caught sight of the old Freh female she'd noticed earlier.

Jilan disappeared.

The crew woman grabbed Lita's arm. "You can't do anything for her! D'you want to die too?"

She dragged Lita through the door. The shuttle lifted off before the hatch had fully closed.

*****

Silence settled over them when she was done, a quietness quilted with the cooing of doves in the apple trees.

"You were full of fire when you were younger," Colm observed.

"My father was a good man — my sister an innocent baby —"

"My dear, you were a child yourself and not to blame."

She thought of Earth's cold-sleep ships traveling below light speeds. The decades-long journey had taken no conscious time out of her own life to reach Earth; fifteen when she'd stepped into the shuttle on Krishna, she was still fifteen when she'd reached the Mother House.

"I feel as if I abandoned my baby sister."

He nodded thoughtfully. "Someday you'll need to go back, if only to recapture your old feisty self."

"That's the last thing I want to do!"

He didn't understand. The Guild was monastic, encouraging celibacy. How could someone like Colm, who'd given up the possibility voluntarily, know the pain of losing family? The short autumn afternoon had slipped away as they talked; now the western sky was banded red and purple and clouds obscured the mountains to the east. Lights came on in the Mother House.

"There's an interesting puzzle hidden in your story," he said. "Something that turned friendly aliens into killers."

"No chance of finding out now. The colony was destroyed and so was the star base. They don't need lingsters on Krishna anymore."

The thought unleashed a rush of relief and despair. The planet invaded her dreams at night, leaving her at daybreak faint with fear and yearning.

"Things have a way of working out," he observed.

He took the arm she offered as they returned to the House.

SIX

Eye-on-Third-Bone-Sixth-Day.

First-Among-Mothers squinted at New-Eye wreathed in cloud over the third peak in the Maker's Bones. The weather was changing, sliding down from warmth to cold. The den-circle they had come to was a poor one, twice times four dens with crumbling walls and threadbare roofs between Smallest River and the forest.

Darkleaf had advised against this visit, yet First would not give in to the body's weakness. She stood in the shade of a Spirit-Trap, pressing the four-fingered hand against her chest, thinking about the Song that told the Folk's origins. There was power in the Song, power to heal the Folk's wounds.

Youngest squatted with four younglings behind the mounded den, a cloud of blind insects hovering above them. First covered her nose against the stench of rotting food and excrement flowing through an open ditch to Smallest River. Only four younglings here, one male and three females. Younglings were always precious, but there were less and less every cycle. The Folk were dying. Everywhere she found the urgency of her task.

Youngest scratched shapes in the dirt with a stick.

"This one looks like a tree. And its sound is like leaves." Youngest made an open-mouthed soughing. "Now you make the sound."

The females obediently made the sound. The male grunted and strained with effort.

A watcher stood by a den whose roof seemed more holes than cover, a thick-bellied male with short legs, arms crossed over a ragged strip of loincloth, small eyes lost in the crowding tattoos. It was no easy task to spread knowledge of the Song among the Folk, and males resisted learning. First beckoned him to join the lesson. He turned quickly, agile in spite of his bulk, and went down into the den.

Youngest pointed. "A special sound, the holiest of all. *Wiu*. It means 'white bird.'" She looked up shyly at First.

A bird's call. The sound Whitebird herself had given shape, completing the Mothers' task. She had been very small, newly under old Stormsinger's protection. For shaping this sound, completing the task, she had been named First when Stormsinger died. Such heavy tasks came lightly when one did not know their importance, she thought.

The day was airless, the sky curdling above the Maker's Bones. Soon wind would rise bringing disease from the river to ravage the valleys and then Great Rain to cleanse the world.

Old Winterbud came up to stand beside her. "Great Rain brings Lost Ones over the river. No more lessons!"

Those who had been lost would be found, and those who had been mad would be mad no more if she could complete the work. Doubt crept into her resolve like a thief stealing grain from a den. Would the Lost Ones listen? Could they understand her words or she theirs? The Folk had been too long divided from the wisdom of Those-Who-Have-Gone-Over, and they in their turn had been damaged by their loss of den and kin. What if the gap were now too wide to cross?

A flock of tiny birds flashed past. She watched them hover over a flowering bush, their shrill voices weaving sound to keep the flock together. The Song of the Folk was like that, she thought as the birds wheeled away, a net binding them together.

"First?" Youngest said.

The lesson was over, New-Eye gone below the Maker's Bones.

"You are tired, First. You could ride. I would pull my brother-in-blood-one-older's cart."

Youngest stood up and pointed to the den where the sullen male she had named by his kin-rank emerged again. Understanding came: This brother-in-blood, older, did not approve of Youngest abandoning the den before she had younglings of her own. And in the way of males among the Folk, First wondered, did he, like Den-Builder in the Song, sorrow that he had not been the one to Go-Over?

Youngest turned to the brother-in-blood. He raised a fist, and for a moment First thought he meant to strike Youngest — I will have him killed if he does! she thought.

He dropped the hand.

First took Youngest's hand in her own and held it tightly, shaken at the fury of her thought. Where had such fury come from? She must meditate on the meaning of this sudden heat.

"I will walk, Youngest," First said.

Winterbud said, "Darkness will be soon upon us."

"I will stay awhile, Mother," Youngest said.

First and Winterbud journeyed home in silence.

*****

First-Among-Mothers dreamed:

A naked male of jutting bone and loose skin. A female wailing, fists pummeling.

She sat up and knocked over a candle. Hot wax poured over her leg, forcing her out of the dream. She had not meant to fall asleep here in the cave of the bones. It must be almost dawn. In the flickering light of the remaining candle, finger bones on the stone floor glowed in patterns undisturbed since Stormsinger's death.

Memory opened. Someone held her. The sister-in-blood-one-older crouched beside her. They were high up in a tree. She remembered the scratch of bark on bare legs. Nothing more.

She gazed at the gleaming patterns on the stone floor. The bone that carried the sign she gave had been a male's. She was not grateful this unknown male had spared her the sacrifice. No matter his intention, he had robbed her. The telling came into being through blood and bones of generations of Mothers, and those who were First led the way. In the dark night she feared this loss would defeat her at the end.

Down the long years she had carried this sorrow, this difference, and could not speak of it. She could not share it even with Darkleaf, though Darkleaf loved her and she Darkleaf in return.

Sighing, she rose and left the cave.

The large hall was silent when she entered, the candles unlit. A thin, early light seeping down from above brought the smell of first snow. Eye-on-Fourth-Bone-First-Day.

Three Mothers, yawning, chopped yellow bulbs to season the morning's broth. Another fetched water from the underground well, water slopping over the heavy pail; Winterbud, oldest among them, still completing her chores each day. It was early yet, the Mothers' lazy movement seemed to say, no sense hurrying. First was not hungry, but she accepted a bowl and sat at table. Other Mothers filed in, the candles were lit, the meal began.

Rockgiver came down the steps when all were seated. The edge of her robe was damp and clung to her legs.

"Great Rain came in the night," Rockgiver said. "The river will overrun its banks before the next dark."

"No lessons for younglings now," a Mother said from the other end of the table.

"Where is Youngest?" First asked.

"She did not return from her den," Rockgiver said, her face sour as unripe *zyth* berries. "The brother-in-blood commanded."

"A brother has no power to command!"

Rockgiver spat on the stone floor. The Mothers averted their eyes and ate in silence.

After the meal, she said, "Find another who can tell signs as well as Youngest. The work must continue."

She returned to her bedchamber and Darkleaf followed.

"First." Darkleaf stood clutching the door hanging.

"Enter, Leaf, sister-in-heart," she said. "Something troubles. What is it?"

"You did not give Rockgiver space to say what she knew." Darkleaf sat beside her on the bed cushions, her fingers stroking, soothing. "A Lost One had Youngest last night."

She heard the words but their meaning was veiled. Then the veil lifted. "I dreamed it, Leaf. I hid in a tree. A stranger's arms held me. A Lost One looked to where we hid."

"Stormsinger protected you," Darkleaf said, her expression grown stubborn as if she dealt with a slow-witted youngling.

"And raised me to become First in spite of my differences."

"Because of them."

She thought about that for a moment. "And Youngest?"

"She will not come back."

All her losses rose in her mind: the mother-in-blood; the sister-in-blood; Stormsinger who had been protector, teacher, and mother. Now Youngest. As Darkleaf stroked, First thought of Rain-Catcher and Den-Builder curling close in the ternary's den, awaiting the birth of their youngling. All the Mothers here had borne younglings; now Youngest would join them.

Darkleaf said, "We have too few younglings."

"I will not speak further of this!"

She had spoken too harshly. The comforting hand withdrew. Darkleaf tucked head to chest in the sign of embarrassment.

"Leaf —" she said.

But her sister-in-heart had left the chamber.

It was better that way.

SEVEN

The silvery words were visible on the air when Lita entered Colm's chambers, but he wasn't there. She gazed at the screen, hoping his work would provide distraction from the sentence she'd just received. Whether or not this was a Venatixi AI, she knew it was by far the most powerful machine in the Mother House; no other teacher had one even remotely like it.

Colm's core list glistened under her gaze, a graph of indispensable words he'd culled out of languages too numerous to count. She drew up a chair and leaned into the sparkling matrix. The words shimmered, a dance of fireflies.

Finger, who, water; the modern Inglis versions ran down like quicksilver on her left. Immediately to their right were their counterparts in the reconstructed roots of the proto-language of Homo sapiens: tik, ku, akwa. Older than Indo-European, older than Sanskrit, the ancestor of all human languages had been painstakingly reconstructed over decades in the twenty-first century, confirmed and reconfirmed by Guild scholars in the twenty-second.

Further to the right were the columns of alien equivalencies for these same words, Frehti, Omareemeean, Tlokee, Xt'la'ti. As her eye moved to the right, the screen scrolled with her, revealing further columns, Gu, Qwtamh, TsSha'sha, languages from worlds she'd never heard of.

She felt the familiar tug of excitement his language study always brought her. It took considerable knowledge of sound changes over time in any one alien language to even begin to see the magnitude of Ursin Colm's project. Many of Colm's colleagues attacked his research as pseudo-science, or worse, fraud.

"If I'm right, the Arm's languages developed in similar ways."

Ursin Colm came into the room and pulled his chair up beside her as if continuing a lesson interrupted for only a moment. The Xt'la'ti word !k came into focus as the matrix sensed his attention. Lita saw it was paired with the Inglis word for god.

"That word has two meanings that are remarkably stable from language to language." Colm pointed and the letters magnified. "'God' can also mean 'first one,' or 'ancestor.' Or sometimes all three."

He waited, smiling, expecting her to figure out what he'd just told her, the method he used with his advanced students. She remained silent.

"There's a further pairing in a statistically significant number of languages for the roots of 'ancestor' and what Frehti renders as 'Sorrow-Crossing.'"

"I don't understand."

"Think in metaphors. The shamans of some human tribes — the Chukchi, for instance — equated the Milky Way with the path of souls. But what they overlooked was this: The galaxy is the source of life, not just the destination of the dead. Chemicals that cause life originate in the star fields of the galaxy. And if we make the leap to metaphoric meaning, the ancestors who are supposed to dwell in the galaxy are gods because life comes from the inanimate stars."

His words disturbed her. What had begun as a purely scientific, comparative study of alien linguistics seemed to have taken an uncomfortable sideways jump into metaphysics.

"Eruditus —"

"Ah. I see you would prefer this in scientific terms." He smiled at her. "Well then. The early physicist Wigner once interpreted quantum theory to mean the minds of sentient beings occupy a central role in the organization of the universe. In a sense, before intelligent life evolved to observe and understand, the universe didn't really exist at all. We are its expression, come to sentience in order to comprehend that which gives us our existence."

She despaired of getting sense out of him. He was a very old man — she had no idea how old. Obviously, his mind had stretched thinner and thinner over the years until holes appeared through which logic slipped away.

"We could call that concept God." Colm nodded at her, his eyes crinkling as if he could read what she was thinking and was amused. "The problem of origins seems to bother the Venatixi too. You see, the 'Big Bang' was a nice little theory, but it didn't answer the real question, did it?"

She avoided his eyes and busied herself sorting and putting away the cubes he'd left tumbled on his narrow bed so she wouldn't have to answer. Outside the chamber's tall windows, the sky darkened and rain slanted across the courtyard. Two young girls hurried from puddle to puddle, their voices drifting up to her as she worked.

"You've heard bad news, I think," Colm said suddenly.

She dropped a stack of cubes. When she'd retrieved them, she glanced at him, gauging whether he'd returned to reality enough to pay attention this time. His face was serious, his eyes sharp.

"Magistra spoke to me. She doesn't even think I'm good enough to be a Guild-certified translator."

Magistra Yauyos seemed to take Lita's very presence at the Mother House as a personal insult. If the Patel family hadn't still had some influence on Earth, she might've refused to take her in. Lita had to admit, her own attitude hadn't helped; used to a life of authority and indulgence, she hadn't adapted easily to the austere discipline of the Guild. Mostly she found it hard to be deferential.

Colm studied her face, waiting for her to continue.

"She suggested that if I insisted on this field, I could find work independently."

"My friends the Venatixi collect facts as we collect butterflies," he observed.

He was off again; perhaps he couldn't help himself. Bad enough that he counted these aliens friends; no wonder he had detractors in the Guild.

He flicked a finger and the sparkle of words he'd been working with disappeared. The pale ocher stone of the study wall seemed to retain an afterglow, then that too faded.

"I've studied them for many years, you see. I first met them when I was a young lingster in the field. They're on a great quest, these Venatixi, and they'll obliterate every obstacle in their way. That's what happened in the war, I think. They had nothing against us. We just happened to get in the way. The question we can't answer, of course, is: in the way of what?"

The far off sound of bells summoned students and faculty to the refectory for the evening meal. The comfortable combination of technology like the AI that displayed Colm's research with centuries-old traditions was one of the things about the Guild Lita appreciated. Her family had known how to mix old and new.

"They're highly intelligent, perhaps the most intelligent species we may ever encounter in the Arm." Colm went on as if he didn't hear the evening bell at all. "But if they were human, we'd probably label them autistic."

She didn't look up, embarrassed for him. The chimes faded away.

"The problem with my equivalency project," he said, abruptly changing the subject again, "is that it's far too big a dictionary for a lingster's pocket where it might do some good. And it would certainly overload any microchip we can embed right now."

He hadn't paid any attention at all to her news. It confirmed her earlier suspicion; he was slipping away into dementia.

"Ah!" he exclaimed. "I almost forgot. On my way here, I intercepted a very serious young first-year student bearing a message from Magistra Yauyos. She wants to talk to you."

Lita stared at him. "Talk to me? What about?"

"Why don't we go and find out?"

EIGHT

First-Among-Mothers dreamed:

A farmer's cart, rain-glistened, swooping over Separation River.

She woke and rose from her bed, troubled. Two days gone of Eye-on-Fourth-Bone and the weather in the mountains turning to snow. Her chamber was cold. She pulled the warm pelt of a cloudbeast over her shoulders and went to the cavern of the bones.

The candles burned low. She lit fresh and studied the familiar patterns in the guttering light. The work had almost broken when the one who gave the last bone did not give the last sound, and the one who gave sound did not give bone.

Yet was not half a gift better than none? First spread her hands in the flickering light, five brown, wrinkled fingers on one, four on the other. I am Folk. I am Whitebird. She made the word-shapes silently, feeling their softness on her lips. Names were words yet more than words. Eye and New-Eye. Here and Not-Here. Folk and Not-Folk. And Human. Somewhere there was an answer to this riddle.

The chamber was cold and her fingers ached. She lit another taper, spilling light over the white bones, then she squatted on the floor and unrolled the skin. Darkleaf-sister-in-heart had marked the signs on this skin; she recognized the curve and slant this dearest one gave to her work.

She knew the words of the rest of the Song; she hardly needed light to tell them by. The weakness of her body had pulled her away from Youngest's telling on that cold morning; now her finger traced slowly over the words of the song's ending as she told them to herself:

*****

The Song of The Folk

The air filled with dust and smoke day and night. Where once there had been hills now there were valleys. The darkness covering the Eye grew bigger. The Folk were afraid. Oldest had no counsel to give. Slowly they saw they must do as the Not-Folk advised and leave Here.

"Here is dying," Night-Singer said to Rain-Catcher. "Go forward. The burden of all life is always to go forward."

The Eye would close and not open again. There were shadows on the land now, stretching all the way to Small Hill and beyond. Below Tall Hill, one of the Not-Folk waited, beckoning them to hurry. Behind the beast she saw a thing bigger than the tower Oldest had tried to build. The thing flashed in the light like water.

Small Hill suddenly leaped into the air then poured down in a torrent of rocks. Where the smallest of the three hills had once been, now there was level land. Dust moved across the new plain. Trembling with fright, she waited to see what would happen next. The dust streamed away.

A loud sound, and a crack opened almost where she stood. Rocks and boulders from both sides tumbled into it. A cloud of grey dust rose from the pit.

The Not-Folk were big and powerful, and she was small and weak. There was no one strong enough to save the Folk. Then sorrow turned to stone in her mouth, and anger filled her heart. The old ways were gone. She must find a new way to live, for the old ways and the old songs held no more power.

Cradling the youngling, Rain-Catcher began to sing her first song, her voice hesitant, then gathering strength:

"The Folk cannot stay
So great is the harm
This youngling too
Is empty inside
But will not forget
The Folk driven from Here."

She walked toward the thing that waited to take her far away from Here.

*****

The chamber was cold as snow, the light almost gone. First set down the skin and leaned back, eyes closed. From that day forward, the Folk never saw the Eye again. And from that day, all males who went over were lost to their den mates as the Eye itself had been lost. No longer the Wise Ones of the Folk, keepers of the wisdom, Those-Who-Have-Gone-Over went mad and were dangerous.

Telling the words of the Song would heal them.

Then doubt entered her mind. Why were not the rest of the Folk mad too? They too had forgotten the Song and must learn it again from the Mothers. There was something here she must reason out. If she could reason right, she would heal this wound. If wrong, she would perish and the Folk with her.

She sighed and stood again, joints stiff and bones protesting. Pain pricked in her chest and her fingers were numb. The Folk had abandoned gods since the Eye closed on Here, for they understood that keeping gods meant refusing to accept blame, and there could be no strength in that. But if there had been one, she would have petitioned for a little less weakness in her body till the work was done.

And how would she meet the Lost Ones in their madness if her body betrayed her? Who would help?

One hand splayed against the stone wall of the chamber of the bones, she gazed up at the rough stone roof. Over her head rose the jagged mountains the Folk had named the Maker's Bones. Had there once been a Maker who made all on Not-Here? No songs remained to tell this tale. Creator and song had vanished together, and the Folk were dying alone.

Something was hidden here, something she must tease out.

I am going mad too, she thought.

NINE

Colm and Lita took the path across the central courtyard of the Mother House, the long way, because the old man preferred to walk outdoors. Heavy rain that had fallen all afternoon had stopped, but the sky was still overcast and the air was chilly. Lights came on as they walked, making golden pools on the wet stones of the walkway. The neat flowerbeds lining the walls were underwater, scarlet geranium petals floating.

"Adina Yauyos and I were young together," Colm said when they reached the door to the Head's private quarters. "Sometimes friends, sometimes rivals, sometimes lovers. Never quite of one mind or heart."

Lita was unnerved by this confession of his past. He seemed to have forgotten she was only a student, further evidence of how his once-sharp mind slipped away. That was bad news for her, for without his protection she would be vulnerable in this meeting.

"What should I say to Magistra?"

He paused, his hand raised to the scanner. "Answer only when asked and display no emotion. Imagine you're a Venatixi."

The door opened. He winked at her and they went in.

Heavy velvet drapes in a dark plum color had been drawn across arched windows, and the room was rosy with the light of a real fire. Shelves lined two of the walls, holding a mix of cubes, small art objects, and a collection of books behind glass. Magistra Adina Yauyos sat in a straight-backed chair by the fire, an Arti's small pad in her hands. She was an old woman, almost as old as Ursin Colm, but the years that had rubbed away his edges seemed to have tempered hers into steel.

Yauyos dipped her head. Colm accepted the signal to sit down. Lita took the third straight chair. Magistra stared at her, grey eyes probing; Lita clenched her fingers together in her lap. She'd been in Magistra's private rooms only once before, soon after arriving on Earth; that interview had been chilly.

"Under normal circumstances," Yauyos began, "I wouldn't concern myself with a client's application. We have regular protocols to deal with it."

Colm nodded, smiling.

"However, there is a problem with this particular request."

Lita glanced up as an old man glided silently into the room carrying a tray full of tiny savories and cups of steaming tea. He'd spent his whole life in the Mother House serving one Head after another. Legend said he'd walked a thousand miles to Geneva to be a lingster back in Magister Ng Lo's time, but like Lita, he'd been too old when he got there. He'd stayed on to serve the Guild he couldn't join.

"You've missed supper." Yauyos set the pad down. "I don't require much. You're welcome to share with me."

The server offered Lita the tray. Although she was hungry, her mouth was too dry to eat and she took very little. He put the tray on a low table between them and went out. Yauyos and Colm ate silently as if food was the only thing on their minds, but Lita gradually became aware of an undercurrent of tension in the room; each seemed to be waiting for the other to start. Colm finished his pastry and reached for another. Outmaneuvered, Yauyos leaned back in her chair and studied him.

"The Guild is neutral to the purposes for which our services are retained," Yauyos said. "I'm not interested in the reasons why any client wishes to communicate with the inhabitants of any planet. Commerce, research, diplomacy, even war, these cannot concern us. In order for the Guild to exist at all, we must remain impartial and nonpartisan."

What a contrast she made with the eruditus, Lita thought; his untidy mind seemed to be slipping the bonds of reality like the pastry crumbs that dotted the front of his djellaba.

"To put it bluntly," Yauyos continued, "it's none of the Guild's business. But I sense something here that is our business. I wish to know if this has anything to do with the Eruditus."

Lita would've liked to ask what it — whatever *it* was — had to do with her, but Colm shot a warning glance and she remembered his advice.

"You may recall, Magistra, that I have a rather fanciful notion that all the Arm's languages come from one source." Colm's eyes crinkled with humor again. "Perhaps this client —"

Yauyos cut him off. "A theory discredited centuries ago. Granted, deep level structures, what we term 'universal' features, seem to appear in both human and alien tongues. However, we haven't found an invariant genetic component for any language."

"I know only the truth words themselves reveal."

Lita sensed sadness in the way the old man defended his project, as if he'd become resigned to never living long enough to see it finished.

"Superstition, Ursin."

Colm leaned forward so that the frayed cuff of his djellaba dipped dangerously close to his teacup. "A scientist must remain open-minded, Adina."

"I shouldn't have to remind you of the First Law against letting emotion color the interface."

"'Through me flows the meaning,'" he quoted. "I'm asking where that meaning flows from."

She'd heard these precepts many times; they were the Guild's Ten Commandments and just as sacred. Yauyos seemed the kind of person who recited them first thing in the morning and last thing at night. Colm, by contrast, had an easier relationship with the Guild's rules as he did with everything else. She wondered how often these two had the exact same argument they were having now — and why she'd been summoned to witness it. Caught up in their own long-standing rivalry, they seemed to have forgotten her presence.

The apprehension she'd felt on the way over gave way to a growing impatience; the Guild rejected her, then expected her to be fascinated by esoteric discussion of a craft she wasn't going to be allowed to practice. She couldn't take much more of this. She was finished as far as the Guild was concerned anyway. Nothing left to lose.

"Excuse me, Magistra. Why did you ask me to come here?"

They both stared at her, Colm's expression puzzled as if he'd forgotten about her, Magistra's impatient with the interruption. In the silence that followed, she realized her terrible blunder. Ursin Colm was truly senile; he'd brought her here by mistake.

Her stomach knotted, and shame sent blood rushing into her cheeks. "I meant no disrespect —"

Yauyos silenced her with a raised hand. "A client alien wishes to hire a translator. Specifically *you*."

"Hire me?" she repeated, feeling stupid.

"Indeed, I share your astonishment!" Yauyos snapped.

Colm chuckled.

"Is this some kind of test, Magistra?"

"Do you or do you not want to work?" Yauyos asked.

"Why? I mean, why me?"

"This client wants to visit Not-Here," Colm said. "I suggested you were fluent in the native tongue."

Stunned, she gazed at him in silence. How could he have done this to her? Had he forgotten so quickly the story she'd confessed to him?

"I believe you grew up on that world. Krishna, wasn't it called?" Yauyos said. "For some reason, the client doesn't want to use the translation programs the original lingsters set up."

"No," she said. "There are too many bad memories for me on Not-Here. I couldn't face it. I'll go anywhere else."

"You will remember, Adina, that her family was killed in a native uprising," Colm explained. "She came to us as the only survivor."

"A day or two ago, you were all tears and pleadings that I let you qualify at all," Yauyos observed.

There was no reason to go back to Not-Here, nothing left for her except nightmares.

"It's this assignment or I wash my hands of you," Yauyos said. "Do you accept?"

"Adina," Colm warned. "Burn no bridges."

His tone had hardened, something in it Lita hadn't heard before, a touch of the bear. She sensed there was a lot at stake here that she would never know about, Guild secrets that went far beyond the surface bickering of two old rivals.

He turned back to Lita. "You have to start somewhere, my dear, or you will have no peace."

Silence filled the room broken only by the chuckling of the small fire. There was unfinished business for her on Not-Here; he was right about that at least. Family duties she must discharge, unpleasant though they might be. She didn't really have a choice.

"When?" she asked.

"Immediately." Yauyos sounded relieved to have a difficult discussion over. "The client will provide transportation."

Lita glanced down at the grey Guild-issue tunic she was wearing. "I need time to pack, and —"

Colm leaned over and patted her hand. She couldn't read his expression but it wasn't the face of senility. There was still something he held back, something of more importance to him than wangling an assignment for a student.

"You haven't told me who the client is," she said.

Yauyos picked up the Arti's pad, interview over. "You'll be working for a Venatixi."

TEN

The First relies on herself alone, Stormsinger taught. Was Stormsinger ever wrong?

She slipped the cloudbeast pelt around her neck and walked through the large stone hall and up steps wide enough for one Mother at a time. A long, long time ago, Stormsinger had led her down these steps, and the man who had held her in the tree, and the sister-in-blood-one-older. Only Stormsinger's face remained in her memory.

Outside at the foot of the Maker's Bones, she stood where icy wind whipped the white fur. Above, bright pebbles blazed, more than she could count, more than all the Mothers together could count, gathering thick in the white road called Sorrow-Crossing. And did every fiery pebble have a name? She had never learned more than the Eye and the New-Eye. Together in patterns, some had names: The Thief, Bird-Without-A-Mate, Two-Losing-A-Third. She had learned their songs as a youngling.

Now she saw this was only a beginning of knowledge. Along this river of light, were there folk like herself, beings who lived and died, loved and sacrificed, and made words to tell their songs? The whole of Sorrow-Crossing was a song itself, a bright river of talk.

Her heart pounded. All her life she had hungered for something out of her grasp. It haunted like a name that would not come to mind when called, this dream that somewhere beyond Not-Here there were infinitely more voices and more songs than she would ever learn.

"Whitebird?" Darkleaf stood behind her, shivering.

"Can you name the bright pebbles, sister-in-heart? Can you guess at their folk?"

Darkleaf spread her hands in the sign of no meaning. "I do not know these words, Whitebird."

"Do you suppose each pebble has a song, like the Song that tells of the Eye?"

Darkleaf hesitated. "What use would such songs have?"

"Knowing this — knowing the names —" She stopped, unable to find words for an emptiness in her mind where the whole shining glory of sky should be.

She saw doubt creep into Darkleaf's eyes, and knew her sister-in-heart feared Whitebird was losing her mind. Was that what this anguish was, only old age torturing her with what had been lost? The loneliness of a life spent among the Folk but not of the Folk, a youngling abandoned and left to die among strangers. Only Darkleaf loved her after Stormsinger was gone. Perhaps she had gone mad from the hard looks, the bitter words. How could she trust the ravings of such a tormented mind?

She pressed her hands over her eyes but the images still flooded, no more real than fog.

"I came to tell you news, sister-in-heart," Darkleaf said hesitantly. "Winterbud died today."

Winterbud, the oldest of the old. This news came as reminder of her duty. She must put away mad dreams and deal with death.

"Find three who will carry her up to the Maker's Bones. I will say the farewell tonight."

"Come inside now, sister-in-heart," Darkleaf said. "You are cold."

She let her dearest one lead her down the steps into the heart of the mountain. But the sky had burned its patterns into her heart and they were not easily swept away.

ELEVEN

They left Yauyos's private quarters, taking the corridor to the outside door. Eyes fixed on the distance, Lita walked a few paces apart from the old man, careful not to let her arm brush against him. How could he have betrayed her like this? He knew her apprehensions about the Venatixi, and he knew how she feared going back to Not-Here. She'd trusted him, confided in him, and he'd used the information for his own gain.

The Patel family had dedicated their lives to diplomacy for several generations; she'd learned early the rule of accepting unpleasant assignments and making the best of them, even when it meant personal hardship. She wasn't about to let anybody know how shaken she was, especially not Colm. She'd try to live up to her family heritage as best she could.

But what sort of journey did you go on without packing? It seemed like a bad joke.

The Venatixi's sudden appearances and disappearances all over the Arm that had made the war so traumatic led to the suspicion they'd found a way to defy the law of light speed. She distracted herself by wondering if some marvelous, shining pearl of a ship waited on the grass for her, capable of warping space so departure and arrival were microseconds apart. Or a shimmering portal under a group of old lindens, a doorway across time and space.

The reality was mundane. A small skipcraft crouched on the flooded lawn, its unremarkable lines reflected in the puddles. No one would've looked twice at it anywhere on Earth. Her father had owned one; Ries Danyo had flown her and Jilan away from the burning compound in one.

Colm reached across the gap between them and touched her arm. "Jas'Alak."

The alien stood beside the craft, tall, skin darker than she remembered from the encounter in Colm's room, more bronze than gold in the rainy twilight.

Her heart pounded. "I don't want to do this —"

The old man shook his head. "You think of this as a betrayal — and perhaps I'm blinded by the chance to unravel secrets humans never dreamed could be revealed. But I believe all of us will gain in the end."

"Easy enough to say, Eruditus," she said bitterly.

Colm looked away.

It wouldn't work; she didn't speak Venatician. Few people other than Colm did; it was a notoriously difficult language to master both in its sound system and its multileveled vocabulary where one word might have several, contradictory meanings.

"You are free to not accept," Jas'Alak replied in carefully correct Inglis.

"Maybe if you told me why."

"A world was destroyed to build a sphere around a star," the alien said. "The race exiled from that world saw a cage to hold the Eye, as they called it. We seek knowledge of how to find that star."

"It might even hold the answer to the origins of life in the universe," Colm put in.

"I don't understand. What's this got to do with Not-Here?"

"The world I speak of was named Here," Jas'Alak said.

"*How can anybody say their own world isn't here?*" her mother had once asked, confirmed in her opinion about native ignorance.

"The Freh don't know much of anything. How could they help you locate a star that's vanished? I doubt they even know what a star is!"

The Venatixi stepped through the open door of the skipcraft.

"Wait, my friend," Colm said. "There's another matter, if you remember?"

Jas'Alak looked back at the eruditus. "We do not forget our promises."

"Ah. Then I'll trust you to bring her back safely too."

Lita glanced from the eruditus to the alien; neither one seemed to care if she understood or not.

"Time to go." The eruditus put his arms around her.

She held herself stiffly, resisting his hug, unable to forgive him.

"Like angels," he whispered, "they never explain, but they don't do harm needlessly."

It wasn't much of a comfort.

Beyond the grounds of the Mother House, night had swallowed the trees and the mountains. Wind-torn gaps in the clouds revealed stars swimming liquidly above the buildings; the incense perfume of crushed geraniums floated on the air. Earth seemed suddenly very precious. She moved out of the old man's embrace and boarded without looking back.

Inside, she found the alien already seated in the pilot's chair, long fingers dancing over a control board that didn't look so different from the one her father had used. She took the seat beside him, careful not to stare — hard to do, because her eyes seemed to have a will of their own. He was really stunningly beautiful in a cold, asexual way.

Webs enfolded them both. The interior lights dimmed and the craft rose conventionally like any of the dozens of skipcraft she'd ridden in. Stupid to be disappointed, she chided herself, like a child who'd expected more presents at a birthday party. The real spaceship must be in orbit somewhere above them, and maybe her new employer had already laid in equipment for her; nobody seemed to think she needed to know the details.

She'd wanted to work, now she would. Better not to dwell on the alien's motives or the location.

New Bombay had been home for most of her childhood. She remembered the DepCom's Residence, the water buffalo woven on the red carpet in her father's study, the little meditation garden with its holo of Krishna, the smell of meat roasting on sticks in the native market where Danyo translated the price of silk for her mother. All gone, burned to ashes. Nothing remained but the horror of memory.

Another memory came back, a scrap from a time before the family had taken the post in New Bombay: Grandmother Satiya Patel in a white jumpsuit, lighting incense before a shrine to honor someone's death, a 'bot gathering up ash as the incense stick burned down.

"How long will the journey take?" she asked.

The Venatixi didn't answer.

They flew through tattered clouds into brilliant moonlight. The curve of Earth, speckled grey and white like a bird's egg, dropped away beneath them, and the line of the terminator ahead grew steadily brighter. They caught up with daylight and brilliant blue sky; then the sky darkened from blue to indigo as they gained altitude, turning to the blackness of space.

The craft shivered.

She caught a sharp smell of ozone — an unpleasant tingle of static electricity passed over her body — Frightened, she turned to the alien —

And blacked out.

TWELVE

Stormsinger had finished her task; the Song turned by her doing into marks on tree skin that any of the Folk could learn to tell. Now she, Whitebird, would take the next step, the step she had prepared for all her life. Then the time of beauty, the time of the Old Ones would return, and though Here itself could never return, Not-Here would become the true home of all the Folk at last. Yet something disturbed her sureness in this outcome, like an itch left by stinging vines on an unwary traveler.

"First!" a voice called.

She turned. A small, bent Mother stood in the entrance to her sleeping chamber, one hand to her chest, her breath harsh.

"You must come, First! Something . . . happened —"

"Why do you interrupt me here?"

Even as she rebuked the Mother, she knew in her heart the flying cart of memory had returned. Cold slid through her as if she were naked as the Mothers dancing in the cave of the bones.

She said more kindly, "Take your breath, then tell your story."

The Mother's words tumbled. "I went to seek — child-of-sister-in-blood. I had — I reached — den circle —"

"Stop. I draw no sense from these words."

The Mother shut her mouth tight, the thin line of the lips almost disappearing. First read the signs: Here was another who was not pleased with her. When Stormsinger completed her part of the work, the Mothers had not understood how long and difficult the path still ahead. They blamed Whitebird that it was not finished.

"A dazzle in the sky pulled my eyes, First." The female mimed covering her eyes and peeking out. "I saw this — this thing fly over the trees along Separation River. I hid myself behind the crumbled wall the five-fingered ones left."

"Humans." She was annoyed by the Mother's ignorance of the name. "Then?"

"I know not."

"Where is this marvelous thing now?"

"I did not stop to see, First."

She had dreamed this. The flying cart that carried Humans returned as the dream foretold it would. This time it was good that they came. She would use their help to complete the work.

"Call the Mothers. I will hold council."

The old female scuttled away.

There was a lesson to be learned from these Humans, her blood-kin that she would see at last. Power came in a flying cart; it would not come garbed in a plain robe. From a wooden chest, she took a soft robe she had never worn. The Folk had long spun and woven bright silk, and the robe had been a gift brought by a new Mother. Yet Stormsinger had disapproved and it had been folded away in this chest. With Humans gone, there was no one left to barter for silk in the market, and the skill was fading.

First shed her own coarse robe. Folds of silk slid over her bare skin. She considered the softness of the cloudbeast. It would be cold in the big hall where the Mothers gathered, but she wanted them to see fully this rainbow dazzle of the silk. She set the fur down.

About to leave her sleeping chamber, she stopped and turned back to the chest. This time she drew out another treasure, a chain of braided river grass set not with clay beads but with polished spurs of finger bones. The bones held a musty odor, part candle smoke and incense from the sanctuary, part shadows of the dead who had offered them. She had made it from bones for a moment she had always sensed would come. This necklace she draped around her neck.

I am Folk, she thought. And perhaps I am mad.

*****

First-Among-Mothers felt their shock break over her, heard it in the sigh of their indrawn breath as her appearance took them, noted it in their head fur standing stiff. Down the line of startled faces, Darkleaf, sister-in-heart, stared as if she were a stranger. It brought pain, this rift between them she had made. There was no time now to undo it; perhaps there never would be again.

She fingered the necklace, deliberately drawing all eyes to the bones. Their expressions marked the horror of recognition. They did not approve; she had not expected they would. The First was the only one who had the right to use the bones. She would give them to her successor when the time came.

"I have made a decision," she said in a soft voice that forced them to strain to hear. "I will meet these Humans."

Pulling the mouth wide in a gesture of amusement or friendship was not something natural to the Folk. They had learned it in the time when Humans built their walled town on the river's flood plain, and they had discarded it again after the time of Great Fire. She did it now deliberately, holding her mouth wide in the uncomfortable smile shape until her cheeks ached, flaunting the difference they had so distrusted all her life.

"We must not give appearance of welcoming them," Rockgiver said, her thin voice a sharp wind through hollow grass.

First stopped, one hand on the long table. This rivalry between them had to be settled. "Why do you advise not?"

"A sign of weakness."

First sat at table, arranging the folds of the silk robe that blazed against the mud colors the Mothers wore. In Rockgiver's angry eyes, she saw the poison of failed hopes. Rockgiver had wanted to be First.

Far from stopping her from what she knew she must do, this coming of the flying cart might give aid. *"When Great Rain blocks one path"* Stormsinger taught her, preparing her to lead, *"take another."* Stormsinger would have understood how two fish could be taken with one lure.

She met the eyes of each Mother in turn, reading in their

expressions whose side they had taken. Darkleaf lowered her head, but her eyes did not flicker. Others glanced quickly away, head fur rippling in sign of their distress. She smelled the sour odor of their fear.

"We must hide till they are gone again," Rockgiver said. "Give them no aid nor counsel."

"It may be that we can learn to live under our stones, jumping in fear at shadows. But I, Whitebird, will not accept this counsel."

Rockgiver held out both hands palms up: No meaning.

"I will not wait to be eaten like a blind worm in a hole. There is more power in one who finds than in one who is found."

"The First has a plan?" Rockgiver asked.

She noted the crafty way Rockgiver spoke. None of them understood or could understand what she had in mind; it was only now becoming clear to herself.

"I will use their coming for our good."

Darkleaf, peacemaker, said quickly, "If you go, First, I will go with you."

"I will need one other." She looked slowly down the table at the Mothers, some meeting her eyes, some avoiding.

"I choose Rockgiver to make this ternary."

Again she heard the Mothers' sharp intake of breath. Rockgiver's company would be a stone in her boot, but Rockgiver would like it worse than she. Yet the Rockgiver could not refuse the First's choice. It was the best way.

"I accept this," Rockgiver said sullenly.

"Good. We leave at first light."

Let them think she went only to meet Humans and send them on their way. When she brought the Lost Ones back to the Folk, then there would be time for understanding. She rose from the table, the string of finger bones clattering, and left the hall.

The Mothers stared after her, the high stone roof echoing with her footsteps and their cries.

THIRTEEN

Or maybe I didn't black out? Lita thought. I just blinked.

The ozone smell had vanished. The cabin carried the faint, incongruous incense of tropical flowers. Something had happened too fast for a human brain to process.

Her hand brushed against her side and she looked down. The jumpsuit she now wore wasn't Guild issue. Thin, silvery fabric, but she was warm enough inside it. When — and how — had she acquired it? Her cheeks burned at the thought the alien might've seen her naked.

The craft descended through cloud cover. Not like the clouds of Earth, these had a yellowish tint streaked with umber as if they were laced with dust or spores. Gaps revealed a planet with a lush emerald green surface speckled silver in the slanting light of late afternoon. A wide, brown river snaked across a plain immediately below.

Not-Here.

The last time she'd made this journey, in cold sleep, decades had passed. Preparing for cold transport was a big deal; you didn't do that without knowing you were doing it, between one blink and the next. If she'd been unconscious at all, it had been for no more than a second or two. The rumors about the way the Venatixi traveled had been true.

"How did you do that?"

The Venatixi glanced at her as if evaluating her ability to understand wormholes or hyperspace or whatever the explanation was, then turned his attention back to the control panel.

She stared out the port. The broken line of New Bombay's ruined wall slid beneath them, stained with moss and lichen. No other sign of the doomed colony's existence had survived the floodtide of vegetation. As far as she could see in every direction, a rolling, verdant carpet covered what had once been the houses of schoolfriends, colonial government offices, science labs, the Residence of the Deputy Commissioner where she'd grown up. All gone now, destroyed by fire and swallowed up by Not-Here's vegetable life. Except for the remains of the wall that once marked the boundary between the colony and the native market, all sign of human presence had vanished.

The craft settled to the ground and folded its wings like an oversized bird.

"The Freh are a race in exile," she said, putting it together for herself more than him. "That explains a lot. And First-Among-Mothers was trying to capture their history before it all slipped away. Danyo knew that. But how can you expect them to remember where home once was?"

She stared at him but he didn't answer. Her irritation rose.

"If you expect me to work for you, you have to explain!"

"Among our people," he said, leaning over and taking hold of her hand, "the young must kill the parent."

She tried to jerk free, but he held her fast, his touch burning her skin. She'd heard stories of the barbaric Venatixi rite of passage involving maiming and killing. She felt like the mouse mesmerized by the snake's gaze and knew if he were to do it, she would be powerless to protect herself. Nor would she want to, and that was more terrifying.

"There will be a moment's discomfort."

His other hand opened, turning palm out toward her face, centimeters away. Something shimmered in the space between them, a delicate vapor inhaled before she could prevent it. She felt a brief tingling, a cool, spiderweb touch. He released her hand.

Heart racing, she struggled to catch her breath. The alien's golden, expressionless eyes gazed at her.

"What did you do to me?"

"We keep our promises," he said.

Her vision darkened. She doubled over with nausea. He grasped her arm, preventing her from toppling.

"Reversible after the work is done if you wish it."

"What . . ."

"You will discover when you need to."

She leaned back, eyes closed, feeling as if she'd narrowly escaped drowning. She said shakily, "Your name —"

"Jas'Alak."

One, or *All*. She understood that his name meant both at the same time.

"I don't speak Venatician," she said. But that seemed not to be true, as if she could if she needed to.

The skipcraft's door opened; the thick smell of the planet flowed in. A small, silvery object slipped out, unfolding itself into a tent as soon as it touched the ground. The alien gestured for her to get out.

She stood on a narrow strip of land between the river and the ruined wall of New Bombay, scuffing her feet in the damp soil of Not-Here, a ceremony of return that did nothing to dispel the frustration she felt. She folded her arms and stared up into the unblinking eyes.

"I understand the necessity of neutrality. But the Guild doesn't insist I be ignorant too. Explain, or I don't work for you."

"There was a race in the Orion Arm, older than ourselves, and more powerful," he said, and she almost thought she detected a trace of irritation at being questioned in his tone. "They disappeared almost a thousand Earth-years ago. We have been seeking them for almost that length of time. We believe they built the sphere around the Freh's star."

A lengthy speech for him. She decided she'd been mistaken about the irritation; the Guild warned that the closer to human an alien's physiology, the greater the temptation to believe prematurely he could be understood.

"You will bring us a map of this star's location."

"How do I do that?"

"Contact the ones Humans named Mules," he said.

An urgent sense of everything turning, sliding into disaster seized her. "Mules are dangerous — Killers. Besides — I don't know how to locate them."

"Your father learned where they could be found. He shared the knowledge with an AI."

"Great! Now all I have to do is dig his computer out of the ruins and see if it still works!"

He ignored the sarcasm. "The machine was destroyed in the uprising, but not the knowledge it contained. They gather across the great river that divides this plain."

"If you know so much," she argued, hot with anger now, "why do you need me?"

The door started to close.

"Wait!" she shouted. "You're not going to make me do this all by myself?"

The craft lifted silently into darkness.

FOURTEEN

First-Among-Mothers dreamed:

A circle of tall, blue rocks. Tree shadow. Sorrow-Crossing.

Waking before New-Eye opened, she pulled cloudbeast over her shoulders and left her chamber. On her knees, one lone Mother tended the cookfire in the hall. Startled, she gestured at First, offering a cup, but First had neither hunger nor thirst today. She went out to stand on the mountain in the wind, waiting for the others. Something had opened in her mind, letting through dreams of things that had never been. She had never seen these blue stones.

Up here, the land was fresh with the damp smell of lichens laced with the thinner scent of deathflower, said to ease the pain of dying if one could find where it hid. She could not take the time to seek it, though she guessed she might need its balm before her journey ended.

A tiny creature scuttled over the rock, iridescent color running across its back, then disappeared. She listened for a moment to the high, pure voice of a stream nearby and wondered at the richness that might be the voice of the river of light overhead.

New-Eye showed on the tip of Fifth Bone. So much in the balance now. A brief day, and too soon night would again cloak the path. She marked the long, slow descent from the Maker's Bones down to Separation River. A very long way, if she were to take the obvious path the Folk used. Stormsinger had showed her a secret path, a swifter way to descend from cloudtopped mountain to rushing water. What would have been a journey of four days would now be done in two.

Darkleaf and Rockgiver came out from the entrance at the top of the steps, yawning and muttering. They carried skin, rolled and tucked into their robes.

She had been waiting all her life to make this journey to find the Lost Ones. Now it began.

*****

After they had walked all day, she said, "Enough. We will rest now."

New-Eye had closed, and the only light came from sky pebbles too dim to warn of cliff and ravine. Her own eyes did not see in darkness as well as those of the Folk; it was not well to continue the journey at night.

Darkleaf and Rockgiver huddled from the wind in the shelter of a rock, gulping breath; age sucked the life from them and often the will. She herself could not stop age slowing her feet, but she had banned it from her heart.

She looked down past crowded forest and a scattering of dens to the thin glitter of river. Still too far away for her nose to catch its scent. Somewhere below where it flowed over the land in floodtime, the flying cart must have settled. Humans returned to dens they had once made behind the wall now ruined. The work must wait till she learned what danger lay in this return.

She glanced back at the two Mothers lying against rocks. "Time to go forward."

Darkleaf and Rockgiver rose unwillingly, backs bent, movements slow. They said nothing to each other or to her. Lower down the path, plants and bushes grew taller until misshapen thorntrees tugged at her cloak like beggars. Rocks stabbed the thin soles of her boots, and wind found each crack and seam in her robe. They walked in silence, Rockgiver limping now, no breath to spare for sharp words. The bushes gave way gradually to thin trees and the night grew darker. The broad-leafed plant called Traveler's Lamp glowed faintly in the darkest shadows, and she heard the skitter of invisible claws.

She would come face to face with Humans at last. Her kin. The thought ran endlessly through her mind: Humans. Kin. Then anger grew again. Humans had left her, a youngling hardly weaned from the mother, and gone away. What had she done to deserve that? Long ago! she scolded herself. Scratching at wounds did not help them heal.

"Look." Darkleaf pointed, finger shaking.

They stood at the top of a gentle slope that gave way to the river's plain. The air was warmer here, already thick with moisture. She breathed gratefully for a moment, then remembering this wind brought sickness, pulled a scrap of silk over her nose. In the river, she could see an island. There Lost Ones gathered in the time of Great Rain which was also the time of sowing younglings. She thought of Rain-Catcher's first mate who had not understood this sowing. Her destiny lay on the island, perhaps also her grave.

Overhead, clouds parted, revealing the sharp sparkle of sky pebbles. By their thin light she saw the ruin of the old wall, a dark, broken scar across the land. Between the wall and the river was a narrow strip of open field. The field offered a strange sight. A den, like a half gourd overturned, but taller, radiant, casting pale gold in a stream of light.

"What is it?" Darkleaf breathed in First's ear.

First's hands moved to the necklace; the bones clattered. She had expected to find the flying cart at rest on the river's bank. This was a puzzle. Light flowed from this thing. What beings did this den shelter?

"What will the First do now?" Rockgiver demanded.

"Rockgiver-daughter-of-Birdcatcher-sister-of-two-older," she said. "I will go down. Have you forgotten the purpose of our journey so soon?"

"I will go too, First," Darkleaf said hastily.

Rockgiver scowled. "The First walks into danger."

"I am a danger to those who would stop me!"

Rockgiver lowered her eyes and looked away.

First and Darkleaf descended the rest of the path downhill in silence. She heard the scatter of pebbles as Rockgiver followed. She stopped a few paces from the glowing den, aware suddenly she had no plan for what might happen next.

Then a wedge appeared in one side of the strange den and brightness streamed out making a path through darkness. When her eyes recovered vision, she saw a tall shape in the opening.

"Who is there?" the shape said.

The tongue was the Folk's, the meaning clear enough, but the sounds were tilted, squeezed together as though the speaker was unused to the taste of these words on the tongue.

"Tell what you seek here," she commanded the shape.

It came further out of the shining den at the sound of her voice, and now she could see that whatever being it was, it was probably female. Whitebird had been taller than the Folk before age humbled her bones; this female was taller than First had been. She was dressed in something that followed the curve of her body, sleek as an animal's skin but thin.

"I seek the Mothers," the female said.

First could not see the female's face for her back was against brightness. Images came into her mind, dim memories of Humans she had once known. She knew fear and anger at this Human's presence and also hunger of the heart.

"Whitebird, draw your knife," Darkleaf whispered.

She touched Darkleaf's arm, quieting her. Fear gave way to excitement. Pulling her hood to hide her face, she stepped forward.

"You have found. I am called First-Among-Mothers."

FIFTEEN

Three old Freh females stood before the tent the Venatixi had provided. Lita couldn't see where they'd come from; there were no Freh dens nearby. They wore shapeless, hooded robes — one looked as if it were white fur of some kind — and had tied scraps of silk over their faces. Maybe the Venatixi was wise to stay away from these Freh; the sight of him would've terrified them.

But that reminded her she had to do this all alone, and nervousness made her mouth dry. Lingsters got used to working solo, Danyo had once told her; this was her chance to act like one.

These females were probably armed, carrying the three-edged crystal knife the Freh used for everything from cutting vines to slaughtering beasts to killing her mother as they fled from the Residence. She, on the other hand, hadn't even thought about the possibility of needing to be armed. Danyo had also told her lingsters never carried weapons; that would've violated the Guild's lofty rules about neutrality.

The humid darkness felt like the touch of sweaty hands on her exposed skin; the river invaded her nose with the stench of rotting cabbage. She felt suddenly as if she'd never left. A warm rain danced across the grass, startling her, and she remembered the monsoon wind carried spores as well. She ran her hands over the jumpsuit finding no pockets that might contain a scarf. There was a small flap of thin transparent material at the neck; when she touched it, the flap stretched up automatically to protect her nose.

She was obligated to take the task the Venatixi set her seriously, dangerous as it might be. The Guild might not think much of her — it hadn't thought much of Ries Danyo either — but she had to do her best. Yet maybe there was room to learn from her grandmother's example and quiet her own demons too. She had no idea how to go about the alien's task, but in both cases, she would need knowledgeable allies before she began.

Her Frehti was hesitant, long unused: "I seek the Mothers."

The Freh females stared silently for a moment as if they had trouble understanding her words. Then one of them stepped forward.

"You have found. I am called First-Among-Mothers."

First-Among-Mothers. A long time since she'd heard that title. The First who'd taken Danyo's finger would be long dead; this would be a successor. The speaker wore a neck chain of something white and lumpy that caught the light.

"My name is Lita Patel. I lived here a long time ago."

"No trust here!"

It seemed unusual for the reclusive Mothers to come down from the mountains; none of the human colonists had ever seen them until Danyo found their sanctuary under the Maker's Bones.

"My intentions are peaceful." No sense mentioning the Venatixi's intentions just yet; they wouldn't understand. She didn't understand them herself. "I come to honor the dead, my mother and father. My sister."

"Mother and father?"

"Chandra and Nayana Patel. My father was —" No way to say "deputy commissioner" in Frehti. "He was the leader of the tribe of Humans on Not-Here."

The old female pointed in the direction of the ruined wall. "Gone in Great-Fire-Burning-All."

It wasn't as if she'd expected to find their bones lying in state; First-Among-Mothers had misunderstood. The most she could hope to do was build a cairn to honor them. She had a sudden thought of Magistra Yauyos's disgust at this example of superstition, but five years schooling from the Guild hadn't totally erased fifteen in her parents' faith.

First-Among-Mothers turned to her again. "And . . . sister?"

She heard a curious hesitation in the Freh female's words, as if she hadn't quite understood.

"My sister too."

"Sister-in-blood?"

She thought of the little girl who'd sung *Wiu* to the note Danyo played on their father's sitar; Jilan, in borrowed clothes too big for her, running back from the shuttle that should've rescued her, and her throat tightened again.

"Her name was Jilan Patel."

There was a long silence. The rain had stopped now and, looking up, she found a constellation she recognized directly overhead: The Thief. Then First-Among-Mothers sighed, an almost human sound. It wasn't only kitchen goods they'd borrowed from the Humans, as her mother had once complained.

"Dead," First-Among-Mothers said.

Not unexpected news. "Can you help me find my sister-in-blood's grave?"

"Where is the flying cart?" First-Among-Mothers demanded.

A moment's thought showed her a skipcraft would be a farmer's cart that could fly to them; they must've seen it coming down through the atmosphere and come to look for it. "Gone back to Earth."

To Venatix, more likely, she thought with a shiver of alarm at where that left her.

"You come to us alone?"

"Yes."

First-Among-Mothers was silent again as if she were weighing relative advantages: One young, fit Human against three frail old natives armed with knives.

"Can you give help? My sister ran to an *amah* — a nursemaid — when we went away. She was just a small youngling. There were —" She forgot the Freh word for Mules. "— others present. Have you heard of her? Surely, someone would have noticed a human youngling."

First-Among-Mothers pointed down the meadow to Separation

River glittering silver under the stars.

Her father had believed Mule territory lay across the river. He'd shared that information with an AI, Jas'Alak said. In spite of the protective suit, she was suddenly chilled. She feared to even think of what must've happened to her baby sister if Jilan had ended up among the ferocious Mules.

"The others, the —" She broke off. It was as if a card turned abruptly face up in her mind, and the word she'd been seeking was suddenly clear. "Those-Who-Have-Gone-Over, do they live across the river?"

"They are lost."

The old Freh obviously didn't intend to be too helpful. Lita understood her reluctance; humans had a bad track record on this planet.

"Will I find my sister-in-blood's grave across the river?"

"Foolishness," First-Among-Mothers said.

Privately, she agreed. The Venatixi hadn't seemed concerned by the threat of danger — easy enough for him, since he was back up in orbit if he wasn't all the way home to Venatix. Why hadn't he come with her if he was so eager to question the Mules? If Humans, a technologically advanced species, found Venatixi to be powerful enemies, what did Venatixi have to fear from primitive Freh? Or even the Mules?

"Eye-on-Fifth-Bone-Second-Day. When New-Eye opens, I will come back."

"All right." She barely remembered the Freh calendar and had no idea where they were in it.

"We will use this night for sleep."

The three females disappeared back into the shelter of the trees. Rain swept across the field again.

She watched till they were out of sight. Second Day must be tomorrow. She accepted the wisdom of waiting till morning; she could use the delay to figure out how she was going to satisfy the Venatixi's expectations. One goal seemed as problematic as the other, but she'd had a lucky break by finding the Mothers. Or rather, First-Among-Mothers had found her.

This First might be as hard to deal with as her predecessor had been with Ries Danyo.

SIXTEEN

"Her name was Jilan Patel."

The words drummed in First-Among-Mother's blood. Jilan Patel. She had never known herself by that name. Stormsinger had never used it; perhaps Stormsinger had not known it either.

She was Jilan Patel. Human.

The three Mothers squatted under a little stand of Spirit-Traps, sheltering from steady rain. The night air was heavy with the myriad tiny scents of plant, insect and animal. First knew these scents as well as she knew her own and Darkleaf's. This was her home, not some world the other side of Sorrow-Crossing. Not-Here had fed her and sheltered her since she was a youngling.

She was Whitebird, First-Among-Mothers. Whoever Jilan Patel had been, she did not exist now. She had perished when the flying cart flew away leaving Whitebird behind. The stranger thought Jilan Patel was dead; she was correct.

Darkleaf lay her head against First's cheek, one four-fingered hand on First's chest in the caring gesture. First touched her own four-fingered hand to the Mother's briefly. Her heart was here and all her comfort, but she would not say this anymore for destiny called to her and she must meet it alone.

The sky was thick with clouds, no bright pebbles showed. Rockgiver slept, mouth open, snoring. First would have liked to sleep too; weariness dragged at her bones. Once she did almost sleep but startled awake at some sound, her eyes flying open.

Then it seemed for a moment that the night shifted, an animal stirring in its sleep, and it was as if she looked down the river of her life at the days left to her. Its ending shimmered in the distance, water fading into the bright haze from which nothing returned.

She could not hush the chatter in her mind: Other worlds beyond Sorrow-Crossing, other folk. And more: The Human in the unnatural den's opening from which brightness streamed.

Human! Her heart pounded. Human. Human. Sister.

Stop, she commanded herself, pressing fingers against ribs to still the heart's tumult. This hunger for days that were gone and those who were dead was weakness. How could the sister-in-blood-one-older be alive, or the years not have marked the sister as they had marked herself? It could not be! All that lived grew old and died. Easier to accept that she was Human herself than that this was a sister-in-blood. One truth did not make a second.

She was rocked by a fierce anger that rushed up from heart to head till her sight went dark in fury. Humans had abandoned her, a youngling, hardly weaned from a mother's milk.

Sudden pain prickled in her chest and down her arm, driving out thoughts of sister and Humans. She bit her lip hard till blood came to keep from crying out. She would not let her companions know how her life flowed away. Gradually, the pain subsided. She would rely on herself and accept her own blame and stay strong.

The rolled skin she carried in its secret place chafed her breast, and she took it out, clasping it in the four-fingered hand, the hand that belonged to the Folk. There was not enough light from the sky to tell the words; she needed none, knowing them by heart.

Rain-Catcher had not shrunk from her task nor Stormsinger from hers. Whitebird would not betray them now. Yet she needed an ally lest death snatch the prize out of her hand.

For as much as she hated them, she knew Humans were powerful. She could not trust, but she would put this one's arrival to her own use.

*****

First-Among-Mothers dreamed:

Blood. A ring of tall blue stones. Danger.

She opened her eyes and sat up, shivering with cold and the dream. Darkleaf still slept on the wet ground five paces away. She looked away from the muted shimmer of Separation River to the mountains behind her. Morning had begun its red slide down from the Maker's Bones, their peaks sharp as knives in the cold light of New-Eye.

Eye-on-Fifth-Bone-Second Day.

From where she sat, she could see the flat, grey sides of the Human's den against dull green of river grass. No light came from the den now, no movement.

A touch at her shoulder startled, and she looked up. Grim-faced Rockgiver offered a handful of *zyth* berries she had gathered.

"Eat," Rockgiver said.

First glanced at the berries.

Rockgiver saw the look and made a noise to show her disgust then went away. The berries were hard, not ripe, but they were the one-in-three that could be safely eaten, and their juice gave strength.

Darkleaf groaned and opened her eyes.

"Up," First commanded. "This is the day."

They did not speak again as they went back down to the Human's den.

When they were still several paces away, the den opened and the Human came out. Sister? First shuddered. She drew the hood closer, hiding her face in its shadow. The Human showed no sign of knowing she was Human too; it was best to be careful.

"Morning greetings to you," the Human said.

An old style of words, First had not heard it in many cycles. Folk who had lived along the river sometimes used this clumsy way learned from Humans before the time of Great-Fire-Burning-All. She frowned at the thin garment the Human wore. Silk, perhaps, certainly not animal pelt. How could this stranger not shiver in wind and rain? She had not known what to expect of Humans, but this foolishness surprised her. It did not change her resolve. She was careful to keep her face hidden under the hood. She had little understanding of what happened here, but she would not allow weakness to lead her into a trap if there was one.

"We will go with you to the island in the river," she said.

The Human looked astonished. First grew annoyed. To come so far with no plan! Even the dullest youngling would have planned.

"Half a day's walk," she added.

The Human drew her eyebrows closer together. Her face folded in some manner. "Is my sister's grave on this island?"

The question was nonsense and could not be answered.

"You are not prepared," First said.

The Human pulled a thin scarf up from her neck to cover her nose against spore-laden air.

"This is good. But you will suffer from cold."

Strangely, the Human made the smile expression. It seemed to come easier to her face than it had to First's when she used it to threaten the Mothers.

"I thank you for your care, Mother," the Human said. "I will be warm and dry."

Rain slanted suddenly across the meadow bringing the scent of river. She turned away. She did not know what to think of this female, and it distressed her to speak. Though the wind was against them, she set a brisk pace, willing her muscles and crumbling bones not to betray her now. Darkleaf and Rockgiver gasped and panted, struggling to keep up.

The Human strode along easily, talking. "My father was interested in everything on Not-Here. He tried to learn about Those-Who-Have-Gone-Over."

The Human talked too much, she thought, and kept her own silence. With the four-fingered hand she adjusted the scarf that protected her nose, hiding the other hand out of sight.

"They raided the colony at New Bombay several times. We knew they were dangerous. But that last time. . ." The Human's voice faltered. ". . . it was the Folk who killed my father, not Those-Who-Have-Gone-

Over."

She stared ahead, unwilling to be drawn into talk of a past that neither carried weight in the present nor lit a path to what must come.

"Why did the Folk kill him?" the Human demanded. "He was a good man. He had no intention of harming the Folk. Was it something he found out?"

She said tersely, "Breath wasted on chatter will not be there for the journey."

The Human's mouth shut tight till the lips seemed as thin as those of the Folk. They walked on in silence.

She stole glances at this tall female, darker skinned than the Folk. Her body scent was unpleasant, thin and sweet. She searched for echoes of this Human in her own past but found only wisps and shadows. In memory, her sister-in-blood-one-older had been a true youngling. This female was a youngling in wisdom only.

They walked, keeping the river always to one side, through scattered rain, brightness, rain again, half a day until New-Eye was as high as it would climb at this mark in its cycle. Her body begged for rest, but she would not give in to it.

At last, wind dropped and rain ceased. New-Eye looked down on them through broken clouds, and they heard the deep, impatient voice of the river nearby. Rockgiver and Darkleaf were exhausted; she stopped to let them recover. The Human female too lay down on the wet land and closed her eyes. First sat a little apart from them, gazing at the river. Thoughts tumbled like startled birds.

After a while, she roused the others and they went on, the river now a raucous companion to one side. New-Eye veiled itself once more and rain fell again.

"Look." Darkleaf pointed ahead to a blur in the misty river. An island rose halfway between the banks, half-visible.

"Leaf and Rockgiver will stay on this bank," she said. "The Human and I will cross."

Darkleaf protested. "We took fish from this river when I was a youngling. We had boats. I know this current —"

She raised a hand, quieting her sister-in-heart. Realizing she had used the five-fingered one, she hid it quickly.

Rockgiver said sourly, "The First walks into danger."

"I have told you how I count danger!" she replied, angry at Rockgiver's continuing enmity. "I do the work of the bones."

She lifted the necklace, rattling it in the Mother's face.

"Bone," Rockgiver said sourly. "Bone is strong but stone outlives."

"At least let me tell of the current," Darkleaf said, hastening to soothe. "A little distance out, a few strokes of a paddle, you will feel its pull. It can take you to the island."

"If it fails to drown you first!" Rockgiver muttered.

The Human walked silently with them a few paces till they stood on the bank of Separation River. First's heart beat heavily in her chest, and she felt lightheaded. The river was wide and flowed swiftly here; she watched the swirling marks of the current on its face and smelled its rich, dark mud. The island was larger than it had seemed at first glance, low, tree-covered, mist-shrouded, and twice as far from the bank as the length of the cavern where the Mothers ate and copied the songs.

"See?" Darkleaf pointed.

A small boat lay upended on the bank.

SEVENTEEN

Five fingers on the right hand. Lita saw them when the old female who called herself First-Among-Mothers gestured to her companions. She wasn't Freh at all. She was Human.

Years of monitoring the planet from space had revealed no broken, scattered colonies, no trace of human presence remaining after the massacre, and no humans had visited since then. It was incredible, yet there she was, a Human.

Could it be Jilan? Her heart hammered at the thought. Had Jilan somehow managed to survive? The old woman's age was about right, but surely it wasn't possible. Yet what other human could've been living with the Mothers all this time; who else would they have taken in and protected? Certainly not one of the colony wives like her own mother who had openly despised them as an inferior species.

First-Among-Mothers turned. The hood, forgotten, now slid all the way back on her shoulders.

Grandmother Satiya; the resemblance was unmistakable. She remembered a ceremonial portrait in the Residence: a white-haired woman in a purple sari standing by the Ganges, one hand on a white tiger. Lita felt lightheaded. Somehow, Jilan had survived. The baby sister she'd carried through the jungle when New Bombay burned was old enough to be her grandmother now.

First-Among-Mothers.

Her excitement was tempered by the sudden realization that more than just a lifetime lay between them; Jilan had grown up alien. The left hand had one finger amputated. But Danyo had given the last bone to the Mothers' alphabet project when Jilan was a toddler; the lingster had brought to an end a custom that seemed barbaric though she understood the symbolism. Why would Jilan have needed to give one more?

Rain whipped across the land, stinging the exposed part of her face. Shapes disappeared; the whole world seemed to turn liquid. They stood together on the bank of Separation River, staring at a low island in the middle of fast-running brown water. This close, her nose filled with the damp, smoky scent of First-Among-Mother's clothing, a smell that instantly took her back to the past to three starving refugees in the cavern under the Maker's Bones, and a toddler singing *"Wiu"* as Danyo plucked their father's sitar. Her sister had never seemed totally human from the start, her milk from a Freh mother, her first language Frehti. Guilt flooded her, as if she'd made a deliberate decision to abandon the child. She owed Jilan an enormous debt for what had been done to her.

"See?" one of the females said, pointing.

Differences between the three became obvious now. First-Among-Mothers was bigger than the other two. There was a different quality in her voice, as though the vocal apparatus that produced it was not quite suited to making the sounds, like a lark's song mimicked almost perfectly by a mockingbird. An ornithologist would notice the difference, or a lingster. Their faces showed telltale differences, too, the Freh faces being broader and flatter than her sister's. They shared expressions, she noticed, a learned thing.

One of the two Freh females seemed openly antagonistic to First-Among-Mothers. Lita understood the words but not the implication of the exchange between them, sensing only the veiled threat. There was a history here that she could never share.

A very primitive boat lay upturned on the bank, a small coracle made of bark and lashed together with vines. It looked as if it would hold two people at most, and risk dumping them mid-current if they sneezed.

"The Human and I will go," First-Among-Mothers said.

Mules — Those-Who-Have-Gone-Over — might be related to

the Freh, but they had a reputation of violence and were quite possibly insane. The island was too close to the opposite bank where her father had said they lived. She hadn't counted on being so immediately propelled into dealing with the Venatixi's task. She'd hoped for time to think up strategies that might give her a chance to avoid getting herself killed.

On command, the other two Freh females uprighted the coracle, then slid it into the water. This took some effort; she watched them, struck by how old and frail they were, almost too feeble for the work. One picked up a rough paddle that had been lying under the boat and handed it to her leader.

She glanced at the swift current and the island. The main reason for going to the island, at least from her own point of view, had been to find her sister's supposed grave. Jilan was living; there would be no grave. Why had First-Among-Mothers offered to take her there? If she remembered correctly, the Freh were estranged from the Mules even if they were related; she'd never heard of one seeking them out.

Jilan couldn't possibly know she'd been speaking to her own sister. And even if she did know, there could be no shared concepts or values remaining. The excitement she'd felt initially at the realization of First-Among-Mother's identity drained away leaving her full of sadness for what they'd both lost.

"In," Jilan said and climbed into the coracle.

The two Freh females hung on tightly to the boat, faces twisted with effort. The current tugged at the boat, and the mud on the riverbank made sucking sounds at their feet. They waited for Lita to follow their leader's example.

"Why are you doing this?" she asked.

Jilan lifted her head. "Do not waste breath."

"You have a goal too. This is not just for my sake." She made a guess. "You need me."

Jilan tightened her mouth and looked away.

So she'd been right; Jilan had plans of her own, something that must mean a great deal to be worth the danger involved. The fantastic nature of the whole situation struck her. She climbed in after her sister.

"Wait." Jilan slipped the necklace of bones off her neck and held it out. Her fur robe slid back, revealing thin arms loose-skinned with age. "Darkleaf, sister-in-heart."

The old Mother called Darkleaf closed her eyes and raised the bones to touch her forehead. Lita thought she seemed reluctant, as if this was a gift that carried a significance Darkleaf didn't want to accept. How little she'd learned of this world where she'd spent her girlhood; it was full of secrets that would never open to her now.

Panting and gasping, the two Mothers pushed the little coracle out into the swiftly flowing water. It would have narrowly held a couple of Freh; two Humans crowded it to the point of overturning. Jilan's gaze was fixed on the middle of the river; she seemed oblivious to the effort the two Mothers were making to launch the boat. Lita stared into the misty distance.

There was a sudden shriek. She turned in time to see one of the Mothers go under in the rushing water.

"First!" Darkleaf cried. "Rockgiver has fallen!"

Lita scrambled to her knees — got one leg over the side — the coracle rocked alarmingly. She could see Rockgiver struggling in the rushing water, barely afloat.

Her sister gripped her shoulder, fingers surprisingly strong. "Stay."

"She needs help —"

Rockgiver's head bobbed above the dark water then went under again. She came back up, opened her mouth as if to speak, but a wave filled it, stealing her words. The current had already pulled her several meters away from the bank.

"She will drown if we do not help her!"

Jilan folded her arms and stared at the island, her expression impassive.

Rockgiver disappeared under the surface. They watched, but she didn't come back up. Darkleaf let go of the coracle's side and wailed in distress. Jilan picked up the paddle and dipped it in the water, one side then the other in turn, heading away from the spot where the old Freh had gone down.

Her sister's callousness shocked her. She stared at the river, avoiding Jilan's eyes. The sound of Darkleaf's wailing faded behind them.

The flimsy craft bobbed and ducked its way through the waves. Further out, an urgent current caught them, yanking the prow around from the direction they were headed. The old woman fought it, her mouth pursed with effort. Lita clung to the side. The wind was colder out on the river; she felt its bite on her exposed forehead. Hugging her knees under her chin, she concentrated on the low island ahead, trying not to think of the drowned Mother.

"This sister-in-blood you seek," Jilan said suddenly as the boat neared the midpoint. She shipped the paddle and allowed the boat to be pulled along by the rushing water. "Tell me of her."

"Jilan." Lita let the name hang on the air for a second. "Her name was — is — Jilan Patel. We were attacked as we prepared to leave. She was left behind."

"By design?"

"No. She ran away at the last moment before the shuttle took off."

Jilan lapsed into silence again, face averted. The current carried them toward a little bay, a thin stretch of beach backed by a dark line of trees. Lita stared at her sister's head where the hood had slipped, revealing a grey stubble of hair, finer and sparser than the head fur of old Freh but obviously chopped just as short, a small detail illuminating a lifetime of experience that touched Lita's heart.

Waves slapped against the little boat, and the wind picked up, soughing through the Spirit-Trap trees as they neared the island. She hadn't wanted to come back; now she felt only a deep sadness that she'd come back too late.

"My sister is alive," she said. "You are Jilan."

"You lie."

"I cannot explain why you are older than I now — it has to

do with journeying so far over Sorrow-Crossing. You are my sister-in-blood-one-younger."

"I am Whitebird."

"Our parents were Chandra and Nayana —"

"I will not listen," her sister said abruptly. "Work to do."

"You offered to take me to my sister's grave, a grave you know does not exist."

"Why have you come if not to help?"

Jilan's tone was oddly bitter. The First who'd sheltered the Human fugitives had spoken of preserving the history of the Freh; what that had to do with the aggressive Mules Lita didn't know.

The coracle scraped sand.

"Out," Jilan said.

Lita scrambled awkwardly over the side, sloshed through shallow water that smelled of rotting fish. Jilan followed, her breath ragged, her robe sodden. They pulled the boat up onto a waterlogged strip of coarse gravel and mud.

"What now?" she asked.

"We wait."

"Jilan —"

The old woman's expression hardened. "I am called First-Among-Mothers."

Lita studied her sister and saw the old cheeks drained of color, the four-fingered hand pressed over her heart. Her own breath caught in her throat at the realization. Jilan was not well. Whatever her reason for visiting this island, Jilan might not live long enough to accomplish it.

"First-Among-Mothers, let me —"

The old woman made a curt, dismissive gesture with her free hand, and Lita stopped. Jilan was used to commanding and being obeyed, not accepting help.

She looked away into the dense stand of oddly named Spirit-Traps silvered with misty rain, and breathed slowly to calm her racing emotions. *"Who knows what slow thoughts a tree has,"* Ursin Colm's voice said in her mind. If any tree had thoughts, a Spirit-Trap would.

Somewhere, down the sparkling river of the Orion Arm, there was a tiny blue planet and an old man looking at apple trees.

They might as well have been at the other end of the entire universe. She feared she would never see them again.

EIGHTEEN

"Now it begins," First-Among-Mothers said.

A Lost One came forward from the shelter of the trees to stand on the island's thin strip of beach. Tall, all his youngling's fat burned from the bones, eyes like flame in the long face, his scent filled her nose with the warm promise of life. Her heart opened to him. She remembered rain on parched land, the smell of flowering grass on the wind, all things rich, ripe, growing, body to body, the rub of fur against skin, the birth smell of younglings. Rain-Catcher's heart opened in her own and she knew a mother's love.

The sound of the Human's indrawn breath snatched her mind back. Impossible to think of the Human as sister-in-blood. No trust here.

She gave too much thought to the Human. Worse, it made her think like one. Bright pebbles scattered along Sorrow-Crossing, worlds where other ways might be true, other beings who lived in them — she hungered to understand all such things. How a cart might fly, a den glow with light, or thin silk protect from rain and cold. How a sister might live so long yet stay so young.

Such knowledge had been her Human birthright, denied to her. It was a song written in signs she had no time left to learn. Impossible things that threatened even now to tear her will from what she knew she must do. Better to reject all than to beg for crumbs. Rockgiver had spoken openly against her, but Rockgiver was gone. The work was more than Rockgiver and Darkleaf and herself and all the Mothers together. Even if all died, the work must be finished.

She studied the One-Who-Has-Gone-Over, standing tree-still,

nostrils flaring, catching scent. His tongue flickered, tasting the air. He moved long hands in ancient patterns she yearned to read. There was danger here and also love. She must learn the way to talk with him.

Mothers before Mothers before Mothers had dreamed of this day when two halves should become one whole. She knew herself the last of this line; if she did not make it happen now, it would not happen ever. The Folk were dying; soon there would not be enough left to matter.

Eye-on-Fifth-Bone-Second-Day. A day of stone and blood.

She looked straight into the eyes of the Lost One, the Wise One who had gone mad, and told the words of the oldest song of the Folk:

"In the far time
The long ago time
The time of beauty
The time of the Old Ones
Water flowed over Here
In all seasons. . ."

She did not know if he understood her words. His ears turned, catching the sounds, and like Rain-Catcher, she finished the song with her own words, making it fit the world of Not-Here:

"Now only New-Eye remains
And the Folk."

She was aware of the Human watching, lips parted as if she would join the song herself if only she knew how. The thought angered. Humans. Not-Folk. By what right did they take what was not theirs, trampling lives and worlds of the Folk? Rockgiver had been wrong. When the time came, she would remember who she was and always had been. Nothing else.

She held up her hands to the One-Who-Has-Gone-Over, four-fingers and five-fingers both splayed. He watched.

"Trust here," she said.

He sat down.

Her hands trembled; she lowered them slowly, not wanting to frighten. The gesture she had used was as old as the Folk, and he had accepted it. A good sign.

Now others came, slipping out of the trees like shadows filling the Mothers' hall at night. They sat still, eyes never leaving her face. So much to tell and so much to ask. So much between them, protection and desertion, wisdom and madness, destruction and youngling-making. Her heart ached, and for a moment she did not know where to begin.

Stiff and in pain, she lowered herself onto a dry patch of ground. Time whirled away, leaves on a river, leaving her behind. She was so weary.

She unrolled the skin she had carried with her for this purpose. Slowly, so that he might follow every word, she began to tell the Song of the Folk's beginning.

NINETEEN

Lita understood this strange, starved-looking creature the human colonists would've called a "Mule" because of his long, horselike face, was actually Freh not a separate race, but it was still hard to believe. Tall, loose skin hanging in folds from his protruding bones, skin an unhealthy milky-white, this one had large ears and small, deep-set eyes. Jilan looked more Freh than he.

He smelled terrible, rancid like spoiled butter. She breathed through her mouth, keeping her breathing shallow. Not every creature that metamorphosed went from larva to exquisite dragonfly, but even frogs were a reasonable change. This male looked as if he'd contracted a terminal disease: Pudgy Freh youngling into sick scarecrow.

Then more Mules emerged, making low, moaning sounds, a ring of these creatures, all as tall and emaciated as the first. They resembled beasts out of somebody's remote past, not humanoids. How could anyone believe they would know anything about lost planets or star maps? Jilan didn't seem either alarmed or surprised. Instead, she held up both hands in the gesture she'd used a while ago. The newcomers sat down.

The words Jilan spoke were not the Frehti of the marketplace or of the female servants who'd taught Lita in the Residence. The language had more levels than she'd imagined. How presumptuous of the first Guild lingsters to think they'd got it all on a brief encounter.

Rain fell again, a shimmer of silver against rocks and tree trunks that glowed luminescent with fungus. The thick smell of rot and decay clogged her nose and she sneezed. She hastily secured the loose flap over the lower half of her face; too late to worry about the spores she might've breathed in. She thought of Danyo watery-eyed and sneezing, affected far worse than either of the sisters.

Once, she remembered, Danyo had held Jilan, and she'd crouched beside them in a fork of a huge Spirit-Trap. Below, a Mule mated violently with a Freh female. She'd never understood this scene, but the story her sister recited to the Mules now explained. They mated in threes, two males and a female, with the male that underwent metamorphosis the only one fertile.

Whatever the secret behind this bizarre event that seemed to leave one half of the male population mad afterward, how could anybody hope to do anything about it? If this was what the Mothers had been trying to do all these years, it had been a futile pursuit. She thought of the old female who'd forced Danyo to help in the cavern of the bones, and Jilan herself, deliberately allowing one of her companions to drown because getting to this place was too important to slow down. They were as crazy as the Mules. It would take more than magical storytelling to fix this.

The Mules howled, responding to Jilan's words.

Something shifted in her mind, like a lens slipping into place bringing a blurry image into focus. An odd sensation like heat haze shimmering a landscape —

I am a vessel, a conduit. Through me flows the meaning of the universe. . .

The words of the lingster's mantra echoed in her skull.

The eerie feeling receded. Jilan's voice stopped. In the silence, Lita heard the murmur of the river.

"Trust here," Jilan said.

Her sister's face was lined with fatigue, one eyelid drooped, her cheeks were drained of color. Telling the story of Freh beginnings had exhausted her. Or was there something else wrong? Jilan was old. On Earth this wouldn't have been a problem without at least a partial solution; life could be prolonged. But on Not-Here, it was an imminent death sentence.

First one, then another joining in, the grotesque beings began to vocalize, a mixture of low moans and high-pitched howls interspersed with yips and snarls —

She closed her eyes, suddenly giddy.

Two Lost Ones reached for her and lifted her off her feet. Her sister shrieked. The rotted meat stench of the Lost Ones clogged her nose, gagging her. They carried her through the trees through shadow, sunlight, shadow again. Rain beat at her face.

Terrified, she grabbed for branches to hold onto, clinging to thin twigs. They gave way. Her skin tore, her hands stung with pain. Then her feet touched ground again.

A semicircle of five, tall blue-grey stones stood in a clearing. The Lost Ones shoved her forward into the middle.

TWENTY

First-Among-Mothers had dreamed these blue stones.

New-Eye fast closing and day slipping away. Blood and stones. She could not keep her thoughts from swirling, eddies in water. Stones and blood. *Stone is strong and will outlive.* Her fingers probed the three-bladed knife she carried in her robe.

Those-Who-Have-Gone-Over made a ring of shadows under the trees, a circle surrounding a circle, waiting. Their voices rang in her mind, sweet as birdsong and as hard to understand. It did not matter. The healing would begin now. The Folk would be One Folk. Misunderstanding would slip away like bad dreams when New-Eye opened.

The Human had fallen to her knees in the center of the stone circle. First smelled her fear. How little these beings that made flying carts and glowing dens understood! Only the Folk could heal the Folk. No stranger could do this.

Stone and blood. Blood and stone.

One-Who-Has-Gone-Over turned his gaze on her, pointing at the tall stone. She entered the circle and squatted at its foot in the manner of the Folk; her bones creaked in protest.

The Lost One entered the circle now and began to speak. A wave of sadness came from his mouth, the sound of bitter loss. The work she had lived to do bloomed in this moment. Closing her eyes, she sought to banish the presence of the Human and think only of the work.

I will understand his words, she said in her mind. I must!

Understanding did not come.

TWENTY-ONE

Lita counted twenty of the Lost Ones outside the stone circle, but there may have been more in the shadows. They were ugly, so tall, emaciated like skeletons covered in rags of skin, yet there was the overpowering suggestion of strength in those gaunt limbs. She glanced down at the sore palm of her right hand; a drop of blood showed where the branches she'd clutched had torn through her fingers.

The stone circle raised atavistic fears of pagan ceremonies, sun worship, human sacrifice, things that had no place in the human world anymore. She saw no altar stone, and she knew the Freh had no gods; that didn't necessarily mean they didn't understand the symbolism of ritual killing. Her heart lurched. Had the Venatixi been warning her of something when he mentioned his own race's bloody custom? If so, what was she supposed to do with the warning? If only she'd taken an interest in her father's research into these creatures, she might be better prepared.

Jilan squatted on the ground, her face ash-grey, eyes heavy-lidded with exhaustion. She felt a rush of pity for her sister left to spend her whole life among these aborigines. What a waste. Frehti had been Jilan's first language; she could've been the lingster. The Guild wouldn't have rejected three-year-old Jilan.

One of the Lost Ones stepped forward. His grey, clawlike hands rose slowly toward Lita. Panic swept over her again. She was probably going to lose her life. He began a long string of harsh vocalizations consisting of clicks, glottal stops, plosives in seemingly impossible combinations. A torrent of sound followed, grunts, moans, whistles.

If she could work out what he was saying, maybe she could find a way to get out of this alive. She concentrated on the sound of his voice, feeling as if she were trying to grab a few drops of the river at flood tide. This was what lingsters must experience in interface with each new language, but they had a whole pharmacopeia of drugs to help them, and an embedded chip to monitor and advise.

Through me flows language — Words the Guild had taught her even as it denied she would ever be allowed to use them. Her mind lurched, staggered like a drunkard, and she couldn't control it.

She screamed.

The world stilled.

Words swam up out of the haze, words paired with their equivalencies —

iK't = ki = water

gta = tantan = brother-one-older

vrh = freh = finger/one/first

Jas'Alak's gift! she thought, then went under again. *Akwa. . . Ka'ka . . . Tik.*

Ursin Colm's familiar lists swirled around her, concentric rings of sparkling meaning. She stood in the center of his shimmering data, as clear as if she'd been transported back to his study. Endless columns of words surrounded her like circles of standing stones, one behind the other into the far distance. Equivalencies swarmed like fireflies. Roots appeared, dissolved, were replaced by others.

The Lost One's words slid through this dazzling cloud, coalesced out of the dazzle: *Qy!q. Ipbk. Iit. Agq* — a stream that became a torrent — *Cq* — *Cp!t* — *Tut'q* —

The architecture of a grammar rose out of chaos. She recorded, sorted, processed, an infant drinking language at breakneck speed. The jumbled, kaleidoscopic shards of language fell into their final mosaic.

The Lost One told a bitter story, partly familiar from the one Jilan had just read from the bark scroll, partly a recitation of more current pain. Famine. A homeworld destroyed. Sickness. Mates lost and dens abandoned. Rage and sorrow. If there was madness here, it was the madness of a race sent into exile and dying. And at the heart of the tale, the shadow of another race, so powerful they could move worlds.

She opened her eyes to twilight, pale stars in an indigo sky. She was lying on the ground at the foot of the tallest blue stone. She didn't remember falling. Those-Who-Have-Gone-Over crowded around her. One knelt beside her, touching her lips with a bony finger. His touch was cold, clammy as seaweed.

The Venatixi had told her the aliens that caused the destruction of the Freh's homeworld were the same ones he hunted. She didn't know what good it would do if he found them, but she'd accepted his assignment the moment she stepped into his skipcraft.

She sat up.

"Draw me a map of the sky to show The Eye," she said in the language of the Lost Ones.

"What do you tell them?" Jilan demanded in sharp-edged Frehti.

The one who'd touched her pulled a strip of bark from a Spirit-Trap tree and held out his other hand. The clawlike fingers were tipped with long nails.

She looked down at the scratch in her right palm where blood oozed and understood what he needed.

TWENTY-TWO

First-Among-Mothers watched the Lost One take the Human's hand and touch a finger to it. The Human's blood sparked in starshine.

Blood and bone — Blood and stone —

The Song of the Folk flooded her, voices wailing down the darkness of Sorrow-Crossing. Spirits of Old Ones, trapped among the strange trees of Not-Here, cried out for healing. And she saw: Her destiny was the last song the Folk would ever have or need, for like Separation River flowing to an unknowable sea, life streamed through her. The ending of the Song was here.

Here and Not-Here.

Through her. Not this Human.

She shook away the tumbling thoughts as a cloudbeast shakes rain off fur.

The Lost One squatted, bending to the fresh bark he had pulled from the tree. Like the Mothers at their work, he smoothed it to receive a telling, a telling written in Human blood instead of *zyth*.

He spoke. But First did not understand the words.

The Human understood. The Human answered.

Sweat stood out on her brow and pain crackled down her arm, numbing her fingers. The words the Lost One spoke slid past her like blood over bones — bones that told the words — *Wiu* —

The work slipped from her grasp. She clenched her fingers tightly, hanging on to what was left. It was her destiny to bring healing to the Folk, not the Human's.

The Human who claimed to be kin betrayed even as she tried

to aid. Not-Folk. Humans. There could never be help from outside the Folk, only sorrow —

She drew the stone knife.

The Human raised her hand to ward off the blade, but Whitebird was quick, lunging heedless of stiff bones.

The Lost One was quicker, catching and wrenching the knife out of her fingers before it could take the betrayer's life. The knife gashed the Lost One's arm — clattered away against stone.

Something seemed to burst inside. Pain flooded. She gasped, clutching her chest with the five-fingered hand.

Then sound and light both faded.

TWENTY-THREE

Lita sat in the circle of blue stones, cradling Jilan in her lap. Her mind seemed imperfectly aligned with her head somehow, an out-of-body experience.

It had all happened too quickly: the Lost One taking a drop of blood from her right palm, making marks on the tree bark which he'd spread flat on the ground, Jilan's sudden attack with the knife, the gaunt figure thrusting himself between them, his own blood spurting over her hands, her clothing. Jilan's collapse.

Now Jilan's eyes were closed, her skin grey and clammy, her breath shallow. She took her sister's fragile wrist in her fingers and felt the thready pulse.

"Help," she commanded in the Lost One's language. "First-Among-Mothers is unwell."

The language flowed over her tongue now as if she'd been born to it. The dance of equivalent vocabularies in the shimmering lists was no longer overwhelming, settling into recesses of her brain like living symbionts, shuddered at but necessary. But probing this richness with her mind was like sticking fingers into a fire; she left it alone.

"First-Among-Mothers is dying," he replied.

He crouched beside her, angular limbs folded under, pale skin hanging in tatters over the sharp bones, and stroked Jilan's brow. His smell was overpowering like spoiled milk and rotting fungus; blood leaked from the wound on his arm where her sister's knife, meant for her own heart, had sliced his skin.

She felt no anger at what Jilan had tried to do, only grief. Her sister hadn't recognized her, hadn't understood. She'd seen Lita as an intruder, interfering with her attempt to heal the Lost Ones by reciting a creation legend. It was a noble quest, only the joke was on Jilan. Myths and legends were powerless to stop racial extinction. Jilan had spent her whole life among the Freh, ignorant of the most elementary knowledge that should've been her birthright.

Jilan's eyes opened; their color seemed to have faded like Grandmother Satiya's at the end.

A dozen Lost Ones squatted in a ring around them. She saw wildness in their small eyes and on their long faces. It was too late for them. The splintered race was dying out and nothing she or Jilan could do would stop this accidental genocide.

Somewhere, up there in the darkness of space, the Venatixi had to be observing everything that took place down here. The One. The All. The coward, she thought, afraid to come down and walk in the dirt and the blood that was real life.

Jilan's head slumped. Terrified she'd already lost her, Lita put her ear down and heard the mushy, irregular thump of her sister's heart. The Lost One who'd caught the stone blade meant for her bent forward, reaching across to take Jilan from her arms; his blood smeared on her Venatixi jumpsuit. She folded her arms tightly over her sister, preventing him.

"Whitebird belongs to us," he said.

Strong fingers pried her arms loose and lifted Jilan. Other Lost Ones came closer, touching, moaning. Their stink was overpowering. Jilan's eyes were closed; she seemed already dead.

She couldn't just give her sister up like this. Lost for so many years and found, only to be lost again — it was senseless, unnecessary. If she could get Jilan up to the Venatixi craft there might be a chance.

The scrap of bark lay on the ground where the Lost One had dropped it when Jilan attacked. Her own blood dried on the makeshift star map, forming a constellation of brown dots. She lifted it between thumb and forefinger and stood up. The sky above the clearing was empty.

"Do you want this, Jas'Alak?" she shouted. "Then come and help me!"

She held the bark high over her head. She'd never hated the ignorant aliens who'd killed her father and mother in the massacre of New Bombay colony, but she hated the Venatixi now. She glanced at Jilan. Her eyes had closed again. She lay so still — too still. Too late.

The river's voice was an urgent roar. Vision shrank to a pinprick. She ripped the star map from top to bottom and dropped the pieces, grinding them in the mud with her feet.

She heard the soft shuffle of footsteps, the Lost Ones carrying Jilan away into the trees. Her sister's fingers opened, and something fluttered to the ground. She picked it up and read the first line of the creation legend Jilan had told:

"The scar appeared on the Eye at the time of Rain-Catcher's birthing. . ."

Jilan was gone when she looked back.

TWENTY-FOUR

The seatweb slipped over Lita, securing her. She sat numbly, staring out the port at darkness. She didn't know how she got from the island in the middle of the river to the skipcraft hovering like a metal insect over the monsoon-swept plain. Jilan had been left behind again, this time forever.

She should've known destroying the star map was a futile gesture. The Venatixi hadn't needed a physical chart. He'd seen it, interpreted and transmitted the coordinates as fast as the Lost One drew them. Nothing so special in that. Humans could've done it centuries ago.

The Venatixi touched the control panel. The skipcraft lifted up silently. She stared out the port, seeing nothing; he'd played her for a fool.

"In many species, such as Homo sapiens," the alien said, breaking a long silence, "culture is transmitted through social interaction."

He spoke Venatician; she replied in the same language.

"Spare me the lecture in cultural anthropology."

"By contrast, what you consider to be culture is for us genetically determined. A Venatixi raised anywhere by any species remains a Venatixi."

She wasn't interested. Jilan hadn't accepted her. There'd been no joyous recognition, no closure of the wounds of lost family, nothing. Just another abandonment.

"Your sister had not been Jilan Patel for many years."

The skipcraft rose above the cloud cover, emerging into a brilliant, star-thronged sky. The Milky Way, white road home, lay before them; Sorrow-Crossing, the road the Freh had traveled to their extinction.

"Why didn't you come with me? Maybe you could've done something."

He didn't answer.

The rolled manuscript lay in her lap; she smoothed it with fingers crusted with blood. Not hers; her torn palm hadn't bled so much. The Old One had deflected the blade Jilan intended for her; his blood had splashed her hands and her jumpsuit.

The Venatixi took her hand in his and slid a finger across the blood stains as if reading something by touch. She was too far gone in grief to fear him this time.

"Metamorphosis is a risk for a sentient species that employs it. In this case, we suspect a specific gene fails to turn on at a crucial time. The cause may be environmental. Here and Not-Here are not identical. Blood may hold the answer."

If there was a chance Jilan's work could be completed — by science this time, not magic — maybe something could be salvaged from this disaster. "Could you take a sample from the Lost Ones to analyze?"

He removed his finger from her hand and studied it. "We already have."

"Thank you."

Something seemed to come into the golden eyes then, a softening. Maybe she only saw it because she wanted to see it.

"Do you wish us to remove the gift we gave?"

"And the information it recorded? Didn't you promise it to the eruditus?"

"We also promised to return you safely."

She touched the side of her head. There was nothing to feel; he'd used some form of nanotech, far advanced over anything the Guild possessed. The thought was sobering. No species was advanced enough or sufficiently wise to foresee what even a small change might do to another. Danyo had taught her that. He'd hesitated to give the Mothers one symbol for their alphabet.

She thought of the argument she'd witnessed between Adina

Yauyos and Ursin Colm. If there was a Prime Cause in the galaxy, a creator or the super-race the Venatixi sought, then Jas'Alak's gift might unleash the galaxy's voices and let the torrent of words reveal its secret. She hadn't wanted to come back to Not-Here; the old man she trusted more than anyone else on Earth had used her. Yet as a result, she owed him the brief, precious moments with her sister.

"No," she said. "I'll take it back to the eruditus."

The skipcraft shivered, the smell of ozone filled the cabin. The view out the ports went black.

She closed her eyes and waited to be home.

TWENTY-FOUR